I0584011

Metaphorosis

July 2021

Beautifully made speculative fiction

Also from Metaphorosis

Metaphorosis

July 2021

edited by
B. Morris Allen

ISSN: 2573-136X (online)
ISBN: 978-1-64076-203-9 (e-book)
ISBN: 978-1-64076-204-6 (paperback)

Metaphorosis
a magazine of speculative fiction

from
Metaphorosis Publishing

Neskowin

July 2021

Singot...7
    by E.C. Fuller

Souls Like Sea Glass...............................45
    by Josie Smith

Free Hugs...97
    by Jennifer Shelby

The Art of Unpicking Stitches................111
    by Jennifer Hudak

The Nocturnals III..................................133
    by Mariah Montoya

Singot

E.C. Fuller

The first Sinmai I ever saw was watching my kindergarten class play from behind the fence. Round belly and stumpy legs, noodle arms, a short muzzle, and nubby teacup ears, lush with wheaten fur. Long fingers that threaded through the chain link like vines. I thought they were a baseball mascot. Yet, even from afar, they had an alertness, a flexibility to their face, not the vacant, manic expression of a mascot. They had the expression I saw on the children I taught and the expression I sought in adults. Curiosity.

They unwrapped their fingers from the fence and toddled down the sidewalk, still watching. The thirty-two kids pointed at them, waved, and called. I also waved, secretly wishing they would come over. My neighbor, who worked with the Sinmai, had told me a little about them, but that was no substitute for meeting them in person.

Then they rounded the fence and ventured towards us. I thought, *Oh no, I got my wish*, and called the class back. The other teacher on duty, Trevor, blew his whistle. Some children ran to his side. Some dawdled, disobeyed, and ran for the Sinmai.

"Stop!" I said in the teacher-voice I had been sharpening. The children halted, and so did the alien. "Back to class. Toby, Jeanne, now."

Toby and Jeanne whined, "But Miss Stacey..." but went. The Sinmai did not move, merely stared, friendly-looking. They were just a little shorter than me.

I approached them and spoke in the voice I used on frightened children. "Hi there. Can I help you?"

"Can... you?" Their voice was creaky and halting, as if needing to be oiled. "Where am I?"

"You are at Zeigler Elementary."

"What is Zeigler Elementary?"

"It is a school for young children."

"What is a school?"

"A school is a place where we learn."

Their ears wiggled. "I may stay?"

"I—no." Their ear twisted. I said clearly and gently, "I can't let a stranger into class without permission."

"Stranger?"

"Someone we don't know."

"Ahhh." They raised their hand, as if offering a solemn hi-five. The back of their hand was furred, and the fur was silky and dense. The palm was naked, pale brown, and rough, and the meaty parts of their palm and fingertips had raised pads like gold calluses or metallic blisters.

"*Singot*," they said emphatically. A frisson ran through my skin. Before I had ever known what the Sinmai were, I had wanted to singot. I just hadn't had a word for it. My attempts to connect with people had been like off-center, too-enthusiastic hi-fives: missing the mark, embarrassing, and stinging. I wanted the feeling of reaching for someone's hand when walking home together, and they not only let me hold their hand, but grasped mine tightly. The shared, unspoken knowing that we wanted each other, without risking mortification and only reaping the rewards of being aligned and connected. I'd felt out of alignment with the human race all my life.

And then I learned of singot, the supreme connection: wordless understanding of a person's entire life.

I pressed my hand to theirs. The pads were cooler than the rest of their hand.

"I am not a stranger," they said.

I had expected—I don't know. A flash of perfect understanding? Maybe our hands weren't properly aligned. While disappointment sunk in, three large men, led by my neighbor Anya, ran down the sidewalk, waving.

"Poche!" Anya jumped the fence and jogged over to us. I had last seen her sobbing on her apartment balcony after her girlfriend had broken up with her, her cheeks smeared with the icing of the cinnamon roll I had brought. Now she wore business casual with a badge clipped to her pocket and a stun gun clipped to her hip.

"Hi, Stacey. Sorry about this. Poche, it's time to return to the lab," she said, and held up her hand as if for a hi-five. They placed their hand over hers, and I realized the hi-five was a symbolic gesture.

"The one called Stacey says they learn here," they said. "I cannot stay?"

"Can't he?" Anya asked me.

I wished I could say yes. What did he want to learn? What was he like? Could he singot with us? "You should ask the school board first. I have to get back to class. I can give you their contact—"

Anya interrupted. "Time is of the essence. Poche, if you really want to go, we can go."

"Yes," they said immediately.

"What? No!" I retorted. I felt irritated that she wasn't listening to me, though I was curious to know why time was of the essence. Yet I couldn't in good conscience let him around the children until I knew it was safe. Poche's ear twisted again. "We have policies around letting strangers into the school. If something happened and somebody got hurt, we would never forgive ourselves."

Anya replied, "The federal government has agreed to allow Sinmai to go wherever they want in Golden to learn about us, so long as they abide by our rules."

"Then please abide by ours, and get permission. I'm not the one who can give it."

Anya said earnestly, "If he can visit just for today, it could mean we learn something that benefits both the Sinmai and humanity."

I wanted to let him in. I wanted to see what he could learn from us. I wanted to teach him, share with him what we did. In my more romantic moments, I thought of my job as teaching children how to be human. Pick up after yourself, wait your turn; if you see something wrong, say something; be kind to everyone... and it killed me that Poche's first lesson on how-to-be-human was to be cautious of strangers.

Reluctantly, I said. "I'm sorry, Anya. The children have to come first."

I returned to class on my own, kicking myself. An extraterrestrial wandering through the streets would be unusual anywhere else in America, but this was Golden, Oklahoma. The speed-bump-sized town made the national news for getting its first stop light in 2015. Ten years later, the Sinmai ship's landing rockets had flattened the stop light. The military moved in and the town had doubled and doubled and doubled. Yet, the first time I had heard of singot was when I met Anya. She had told me, through hiccups and tears on our apartment balcony, that she was the Director of Xenologic Studies at the Interplanetary Institute.

"Oh, wow!" I had said, "What's that like? Did you get to meet the Sinmai? Can they really read minds?"

"Yes and no. We're not sure what's going on. When they align the pads on their fingers and palms, they share information as pure experience. They call it *singot*. A moment where they share what it's like to be them. For example, if I wanted to singot—" she pressed her hands together "—what I did with you with my colleagues, I would pass on the sensory memory of your voice, the taste of the cinnamon roll, what I felt, what we said... We think it's a perfect transmission of information.

"But singot only works in person. Their technology can't support the volume of information needed to replicate singot or even substitute for it. Also, they must singot to stay healthy, and they need many Sinmai to singot with." Anya wiped her tears away with the heel of her hand. "Six is the smallest number of Sinmai who can singot for extensive periods of time without falling physically or mentally ill. They have a spoken language, but with a limited vocabulary. They think their language evolved so they can signal to each other that they want to singot. They want to learn language as an alternative to singot so they can explore the galaxy farther than they have before."

"I wish I could singot," I said fervently. "That would be amazing."

"That's why we're helping them. We're studying their behavior and anatomy to understand how they do it. In fact, they killed a crew member and gave us their body." My stomach lurched as she went on. "In this case, the one they killed had gone insane. They wouldn't singot with the rest of the crew," she answered my question before I asked it.

"That's..."

"They think of individuality differently than we do," she said, wiping her face. "Why do you want to singot?"

"Why wouldn't I?"

The question was both rhetorical and not. Sometimes I felt like I was hatched from a locker. Born to teach and nothing else. If I could compare my inner life to someone else's, I could understand why I felt different.

Questions pelted me when I slipped back into class.

"Where did the alien go? Is he here? Can we see him?"

Trevor jumped in. "Why don't we start our activity? Paint your favorite memory."

They groaned, but they pulled on their smocks and got busy smearing paint over their paper. If Sinmai were to study pictures drawn by children and took them to be an accurate picture of human life, they would be very, very wrong. Jeanne painted something that could be a dog or a cat or a cow—it had four legs and black and white spots and a bottle-brush tail. I wondered if Poche knew what those animals were.

Trevor gasped. Behind the window of the classroom door, Poche's big golden head loomed. Anya came in, followed by the men, Poche, and the superintendent. The kids gaped. Some ducked behind their canvas.

"We got permission," Anya told me, a little smugly.

The superintendent motioned me closer and said in an undertone, "I said he could

15

watch and participate, but he can't touch the children or be alone with them. And one of the teachers has to be with him at all times."

I forced myself to take steadying breaths and to think deliberately. My eagerness to see what would happen warred with my conscience. How well did Poche understand human speech? Did he understand what we were asking of him?

I said to Poche, "Do you understand the rules?"

"Yes," he said. "Can't touch. Can't be alone."

"And?"

"And a teacher has to be with me."

Think of him as one of the students, I told myself. I took a breath. "Okay." I addressed the class. "Everyone? Poche will be joining us in class today. Let's give him a big welcome!"

"Hi, Poche!" they chorused. The enthusiasm made his fur flare.

"We are painting our favorite memory," I explained to him. "Do you want to try?"

"Yes."

I tied an apron around Poche's belly, handed him a paintbrush, and stood a blank easel with a big sheet of paper before him. "Jeanne, can you share your paint and water with Poche?"

"Yes." She scooted her easel over, shyly.

"Thank you, that's very nice of you. Could you show Poche how to paint?"

"Yes." Jeanne grabbed her brush, dipped it in water, and scrubbed it against the red paint. She poked her canvas a few times. "Like that."

Poche scrutinized the other paintings for a minute. At last, he swirled his brush in blue, and swept it in a circle over the canvas. Anya took notes while one of the men with her recorded Poche on his phone. Poche filled in the blue with patches of deeper blue, then green.

"Is that Earth?" asked Jeanne.

"Yes." More confidently, he loaded his brush with grey and drew a rectangle around Earth, then painted a yellow and brown figure at the bottom of the rectangle. He switched to red, and dabbed dots in a square outside the rectangle.

"Controls," he said.

"Spaceship!" said a little voice at my hip: Toby. The rest of the children abandoned their easels to ogle as Poche swept color across his canvas.

"Yes." He dabbed buttons in other colors and added squiggles—wires?—and added the ears and tails to the figures.

I asked, "Poche, would you share your memory with the class?"

"The memory is..." His fur slicked down and his eyes dilated, scanning blankly, as if searching the wrinkles of his brain. Other than his eyes, he was as still as a tree. At last, he said, "...not... enough... words."

"That's okay," I said. "That's what we learn in kindergarten. Words, and how we use them with others."

A few hours after he was led out of the school, the paperwork was signed, and the Institute rigged the classroom with cameras and microphones and sensors. Every interaction, every word, would be recorded and catalogued.

The next day, Anya hunched in a chair so small her knees practically hit her chin. Like the other kids, Poche had his own cushion, forest green corduroy to contrast with his flaxen fur. Anya looked around the room with a soft, wistful expression I often see on visiting adults without children.

The kids streamed in. When some saw Poche, they gasped and waved. Davy spotted him and dashed back to his mom, burying his head in her thigh. She unwrapped his arms from her leg.

Before we began class, we explained to the children what was going on and allowed them to pepper Poche with questions. Hands rocketed into the air.

"Why did you come to Earth?"

"What is your home planet called? What is it like?"

"Do you like it when we call you alien? Do you want to be called something else?"

Poche answered each question with an air of polite interest. I kept my hands in my lap, though I had a billion questions myself.

For our first exercise, Trevor and I asked the children about their weekend.

Janice's hand zipped into the air. "I wanna share!"

"Okay, Janice, go ahead," I said.

Janice recited, "I went to the recycling center with Mommy. We recycle everything. We got ice cream after. Daddy wasn't home and I sat in his chair. Angela licked my feet. The end."

"Who's Angela?" I asked.

"My cat."

"Excellent. Who's next?"

More hands. One was Poche's.

I called on him.

He said, "I woke when your side of the planet faced your central star, at the time you call 7:46:36 AM central time, in the mothership, in what humans call my 'bed', from a dreamless, 8.96-hour-long, oxygen-supplemented… thing we do at night?"

The children giggled.

"Funny?" he asked.

I explained, "You don't have to explain every little detail, Poche."

"But that was the weekend."

"We aren't trying to explain the whole weekend. We are sharing the most memorable things that happened during the weekend. What is the essence of the weekend?"

One of his ears twisted. "All of the weekend."

Anya wrote frantically, tearing the paper of her legal pad in her haste to flip to a new page.

"Homework for you," I said to Poche. The children tittered. "Five sentences. No longer than ten words each."

Both ears twisted and his fur frizzed.

"It's doable, I promise," I said. "You don't have to do it now."

He twisted one ear and replied, "Not enough words."

I pulled a beginner's dictionary from the bookshelf and handed it to him. "This is a dictionary," I said. "It will help you understand where words came from, how they are pronounced, and what they mean."

After that, he carried the dictionary around like a blanket. He only set it down at recess to watch the class shout and play. Anya explained games to him: Red Rover, tag, hide and seek, kickball. Mesmerized, he watched the children with the intense stare of a baby as they weaved, collided, argued, cooperated, and ran back and forth across the grass.

"How do they know how to…?" He trailed off. Then he riffled through the dictionary.

The kids pulled him into their games, but he could only stand, puzzled, as the kickball whanged off his belly. After the first brutal game, Kai ran up to him and hugged him.

"I'm sorry," he said. "I love you."

Poche merely said, "It's okay."

At the end of the day, Anya, Poche, and I stayed behind in the empty classroom to go over the day. I saw him turn to the page defining *love*. Anya had stepped out into the hall to have a phone call about confidential Institute stuff, and he and I were alone.

I said, "I don't think the dictionary will help you understand every word."

"Why not?" he asked.

"Sometimes things need to be experienced to be understood. But," I mused, "not everything can be experienced by everyone. Otherwise, there would be no need to communicate."

"Like *abai*?"

"What's abai?"

"Abai is..." His fur slicked down. After a long moment, he said haltingly, "Abai... is... when you don't singot. It makes one..." Poche flipped through the dictionary again, and he did not finish his sentence.

"Like loneliness," I suggested. "A fatal loneliness."

Poche flipped to both words. His ears wiggled. "Yes!" he said. "Some yes."

"Is there a cure for being abai?"

"Singot."

"Like loneliness," I repeated. "Our species are somewhat alike."

"What is the cure for loneliness?"

"Talking or writing to someone could help," I replied. "If the lonely person is honest. But sometimes they don't know what they need to hear. Or say." I hesitated. "I'm in that situation now."

"You need to singot," Poche said authoritatively.

"Agreed."

"Ergh." Poche drummed his fingers and his ears swirled. He looked like he was winding up for something serious. "You may die soon."

"No, I won't," I said, alarmed. "Humans can die from loneliness, but not that easily. Sometimes it can take years. Decades." *Oh God, decades?* said a little voice in the back of my mind.

Poche relaxed.

Anya returned. Her mouth was pulled tight as she set her phone down on the table to record. "Poche, tell us what you thought about today's events."

"What is love?"

I caught Anya's eye and hummed the famous bars from the song. Anya smirked.

She said, "Love is when you feel deep, tender affection for someone. Like how I loved my girlfriend. But it doesn't mean they will feel the same way."

"There're different kinds of love," I said hastily. "And none are less than others. Love for your partner, your parents, your friends, your children, your country—"

Anya cut in, "But the Sinmai don't have to worry about attraction getting in the way. They're all asexual. They don't experience sexual attraction, whatsoever."

I felt a strange internal fracturing, like an ice cube dropped in water.

Poche asked, "Then what is love for?"

I answered, quietly, "Love, I think, makes up the gap between language and understanding. People misunderstand quite often. Sometimes they don't listen. But, if they love each other, they can trust the other person and assume the best intentions from what is said." As I spoke, the fracturing traveled along my nerves and blood vessels. An odd sensation of horror—and relief. *Asexual.*

Poche flipped through his dictionary to 'misunderstand,' 'trust', and 'intentions.' He curled his hands into fists as he scanned the words.

Anya asked him, "What are you thinking?"

"I think I see now," he said. "Sinmai failed to use language correctly before. Yuche said they went abai on purpose. They said we had to... risk it. To test language." He turned the dictionary's pages to the word *risk*. "We did not believe them. And now there are six of us." He opened his hands. "I am thinking, what did Yuche think? They did not have the words that I have now."

Poche's hands clenched briefly, crumpling the page, and he smoothed the paper.

"If... language... can..." He put his hands together. "Singot. It can also..." He took his hands apart. "Stop abai."

"But you don't need to be abai to singot," Anya said.

"You need to be a little abai to singot," Poche replied. "Otherwise... why singot? That's why, I think, Yuche went abai. We... did not...." His mouth worked for a moment before he managed, "Trust."

My heart clenched for the Sinmai. Poche turned the dictionary to the first page of the 'A' section.

"I will need more words," he said. "I will test language, and go abai."

I passed a park, walking from my kindergarten to my apartment, and a couple relaxing on a picnic blanket under a tree. The woman leaned close to the man, laughing, and I could not ever remember being so radiant. *How are they doing it? What does it mean when she looks at his hands, what does it mean when he rolls up his sleeves, what is he doing to her that makes her beam like that? What does it feel like for both of them?*

Was this how Poche felt living with humanity? I thought, *Singot is better. Why articulate something to somebody else when you can just feel it together?* It made sense why the Sinmai would be asexual.

Yet that thought disturbed me. It couldn't be right.

I shut myself in my apartment and researched asexuality.

As I read articles, forums, papers, I felt myself draining into a deadly swallowing sea without bottom. My past felt empty, even as I questioned the emptiness, hoping something would answer back. I thought I had been in love before. A middle-school friend, a sleepover. The lights going out as if snatched away by the lightning storm that rolled in. As I groped for a light switch, I had found a hand. We screamed, then burst into laughter, grabbed again, and caught each other. We were as close as a pair of socks. I'd felt this time and again with others, believing that the urgent wanting (as I imagined sexual desire would feel) would come sometime for the right person. I wanted a light switch or a hand to hold. I tried to imagine sex, and couldn't.

The websites I found emphasized that asexuality didn't mean that you couldn't give or feel love. Asexuality had little to do with the lack of communication. At least, the kind of communication Poche sought. Yet, asexuality felt important to abai and singot, and I couldn't explain why.

I couldn't wait for humanity to invent something that would allow us to singot. Poche was right; language would have to suffice. But the dictionaries wouldn't be enough, because it wasn't just the lack of words—what words we didn't have could be invented. It was the lack of trust that someone else would understand you and be patient with you while you fumbled to explain yourself. But how could he learn patience when he didn't have the time? How long could a Sinmai be abai until they died?

The following day, when going over vocabulary with Poche, he said, "Yesterday, you reacted to Anya's words."

A pit deepened in my stomach. Anya was taking notes beside us. Her eyebrows quirked.

"Uh, yes." I had sworn that I would be honest with children when they asked me questions, and I counted Poche as one of them. "About love. She accidentally touched on something I had been thinking about for a long time."

"What is it?" he asked.

"I'm still thinking about what it means. How to say it." I asked, "Can I tell you later when I know more about how I feel?"

His lips lifted. His gums were black and set with chisel-like teeth beveled to sharp edges. I imagined the crew mate who had been sacrificed. "Abai, Stacey," he said. "That's abai."

He held up his hand suddenly, and I jumped, as if he had been about to slap me. "You will tell me?"

I put my hand to his. "I promise."

Poche flipped to the word 'promise.' He looked mollified, but still suspicious.

"Very good," Anya said, scrawling notes at light speed. "Very interesting stuff."

As class went on, I thought, *Maybe I should have just told them. Why didn't I want to?* Maybe it was because it seemed pretty hasty to tell people I was asexual so soon after discovering it myself. What if I was wrong? I wanted to be wrong. I was delaying for evidence to the contrary: a leaping heart at another person's appearance, an undeniable feeling between the legs. When I thought of a partner, I pictured myself standing next to a blot, like someone had put their thumb over a camera lens.

But it wasn't just that. I was like Tasha, who always could be found hovering outside play groups, waiting to be invited in. I always stepped in to help her. But now I wondered whether I needed an adult to do that for me with other adults. *But* I'm *an adult, damnit. I should be able to do it myself.*

We stayed behind after class to go over the day, as usual. Anya had brought a bag of clementines and the sweet lobes glowed in the sunlight. Her hand knocked against mine repeatedly as we reached for them. Each time it was like the tongue of a bell resonating through me. As I put a lobe in my mouth, I forced myself to imagine it was her ear. The smooth, plump crescent, warm, tart, bursting.

And then I thought, *What am I doing?*

Anya caught my eye with her deep brown gaze.

Poche said gravely, "Stacey, you are red. Why?"

"Oh, hush." I was mortified, smiling awkwardly. I hadn't thought he would notice.

"You can't say that to him." Anya smiled with crinkling eyes.

"Noooo, I'm not going to say." I was laughing, even as she grabbed my hands. I was half-serious. She was getting the wrong idea. But the contrarian part of me said, "Yes, yes, yes." Where would this go? *Don't you want to know her more? Even if it starts with a misunderstanding?*

"You have to explain, or he won't know." She beamed like the sun. Nobody had ever looked at me like that before. I wanted to blind myself looking.

Both of his ears twisted.

He asked, "Why will you not tell me?"

"Well…" I couldn't answer. I didn't have an answer, at least, not one that I wanted to say out loud. Anya was listening. *Say it*, I thought. "I'm red because I'm sunburned," I said lamely. *Such a coward*, I thought. Breaking my pledge not to lie to children so I didn't have to confront difficult things. Anya raised an eyebrow.

Poche asked, "Why do you say that?"

Anya said icily, "Sometimes, Poche, people are uncomfortable with same-sex flirting."

"I'm not uncomfortable!" I protested.

"Then why don't you explain?"

"Why don't you explain, Anya?" he asked. "Is this a power struggle?"

"No," Anya and I said together.

He asked, "Is there danger nearby? And redness is camouflage?" I chuckled. Anya blistered me with a look. "Is it a secret? Is it like how Sinmai treat *horkew'e* ceremonies, during which we send a young Sinmai into the *threwd* with *sled*, *vie*, and *wave*—"

"Poche," I said.

But he babbled, "—and we tell them, 'Go. Make yourself abai, see how plants go together, how water unmakes itself from clouds, and when you return, singot, and you will know Sinmai and know nothing and they will go out and grow abai with only two hands—"

Anya had pulled out her phone and dialed frantically. Was he going insane? Was this abai? I held up my hands. Fuck my feelings, I'd deal with the fallout with Anya later. But then his fingers wrapped twice around my hand and squeezed. It was like being caught in a machine—flesh bending too far in wrong ways.

I screamed, "I will tell you! Please, let go!"

He yanked his hands away as if he had touched a scorching stove. "I am sorry. Sorry. Sorry."

My heart raced in my throat. My joints cracked, and welts crossed my wrists.

Anya had pulled out her stun gun. When she saw my expression, she shoved it back in its holster.

"Let's end here," she muttered.

Poche's hands flexed and flexed, as did mine. Anya's clenched.

What would have happened if I had been honest? I had been... But I *didn't* know why I had blushed. I thought I was asexual. Right?

Idiot, I told myself. *Language only works if you use it.*

I didn't understand what had happened to me. I thought that if I could just explain what I felt to myself, I would understand. Then I would know what to say to Poche and Anya. I had to know perfectly. Otherwise, it would feel like I was lying to them.

But the contrarian inside me said, *You won't know perfectly. What are you afraid of?*

My answer was meager, pathetic. *I'm afraid they won't believe me.*

And then I felt angry with myself. *How will Poche learn how to trust if I'm not a good role model? I have to tell him soon*, I told myself. *Even if I'm not sure what it is, even if I stammer or stutter. He's trying. Meet him half-way. This I can do for him.*

A storm muscled into the following morning's blue sky. Trevor led the group in a lesson about the water cycle, how clouds form and rain falls. Poche watched the sky with a finger tapping his knee.

The lights flickered.

"It's okay, everyone," said Trevor. "We have our flashlights."

Then thunder shattered the air and the lights went out.

Children screamed. Trevor switched on his flashlight and called for order. The grey-blue disturbed light from the window was all we had, and the flashlights—and Poche, whose hands glowed. A pale blue light emitted from his calluses.

"Poche, how are you doing that?" Anya asked, and held out the recorder.

"The Sinmai evolved to singot," he said. His hands clenched, as if to crush the light. "The ship will be here soon."

The way he sat, the way he looked out the window, the tapping. Something else I couldn't understand.

"Poche?" I said uncertainly.

"Let's go out to the hall," Poche said suddenly, rising.

The hall was dark, except where the storm's light wavered through the windows. The gloom shied away from Poche's upheld hands.

"I have discovered something about the nature of abai," Poche said. In the dark, he looked misshapen, bestial. "Abai is not a disease. It is a stranger-maker, an evolutionary learning mechanism which —" He vibrated. "Which singot overrides." Suddenly, he said, "Do not let the others singot with me, Stacey. Explain to them. I promise I will tell them. I need to stay abai, just for a little while longer—it's the only way to test—"

His words jumbled together.

"Stacey, get away from him," Anya said. She reached for something on her belt, and there was an electric whine.

I said, "Tell me—what's wrong?" I raised my hand.

"Poche, walk in front of us to the lobby," said Anya.

"Anya, wait. I'll take full responsibility."

"For what?" she said tersely.

"Poche, I'll tell you—the thing I didn't want to talk about..." My heart clogged my throat. "The word that I reacted to—what Anya said—about asexuality. I have always felt a little... out of alignment, with people, all my life. When she said that, I realized I was... asexual. And my life made sense." Poche's fur stood on end. "But it scared me, because I didn't know what the rest of my life would look like."

Poche's expression was like none I had ever seen on Earth. He said in a garbled voice, "I don't understand."

I felt like he had reached inside my chest and crushed my heart.

The stormlight dimmed, and so did the slashing of the rain on the windows. Beyond the lobby, over the parking lot, was something that could only be the Sinmai ship. Like a black moon had descended from the sky and blocked the rain. Sirens keened, approaching.

Poche hurried out of the lobby into the rain. From the ship, five Sinmai descended on a platform. The way they glanced around themselves, their gestures, the way they stood—like five fingers on the same hand. Poche approached them and spoke rapidly in Sinmai before they could. He overpowered their attempts to cut in, repeating *abai* and *singot* amidst a torrent of English and Sinmai words. The five exchanged a complicated set of gestures like a secret handshake. Blue sparks danced between their palms like a cloudless summer day, when you can see infinity hinting beyond the sky. Poche shivered. But he stepped away, covered his eyes, and said something in a breaking voice.

The Sinmai lunged for him. They wrestled him down as military vehicles skidded round the corner. Their powerful lights caught the tussling aliens and obliterated individual features. Snarls juddered from Poche's chest. Claws extended from his feet and gouged earth from the lawn. One Sinmai had bit down on his arm with those teeth and another champed his leg, forcing him down.

Tears smeared my vision. I felt divided against myself. *Help him! Leap in, say something! Why don't you do anything? Something!* But what could I say that could replace singot? I had already failed.

The lead Sinmai pinned down Poche's arm, uncurled his clenched hand, and pressed their palm to his.

Light annihilated the schoolyard. When I recall that moment now, it is like a still in a movie, and a bomb has just gone off. It doesn't seem like it happened. I should have felt the blast like a ghostly wall. I know the soldiers who had been running to confront the Sinmai recoiled. I know the Sinmai pile fell apart. I saw one fall to the side, on the road, making an awful scream like an iceberg splitting.

And I saw that Poche lay still. Clearest of all was a black asterisk of soot on the asphalt where his hand should be, and his wrist cuffed with flames.

Next week, kindergarten resumed. I told the class that Poche might not come back. We all cried for a while. I put his painting on the wall so parents and children could see it with the rest of the class. We didn't know if he would come back, but we had to keep going like he would. We set out his floor cushion and put it away at the end of each day. I felt like an extra chamber had been carved out of my heart and my blood had leaked away, and I was only still moving because I was too numb to realize I had died. If only I had had better words and put them in a better order. If only I had told him sooner, he would be alive.

But then he returned.

Certainly, it was a Sinmai, toddling down the sidewalk on the other side of the fence, the stub of an arm bandaged. Children screamed and ran towards him, and Trevor and I ran to call them back. Trevor called, at least—I just ran. Poche waded into the children and they glommed onto him. Anya and the guards who followed him stepped away. Anya looked tense, expectant.

"Good morning," Poche said to me. "I'm sorry."

"We're all just glad you're okay," I said through a tight throat.

"No," he said emphatically. "*I'm* sorry. Poche has died. This body is now Oche."

The children quieted. *Poche has died. This body is now Oche.* These words did not go together with what I saw. They stood straighter. Their speech was clearer. They had Poche's body. Yet, I was looking at a stranger.

To me, Oche held up his hand. With trepidation, I placed mine over it.

"When we singot," he said carefully. "We pour ourselves together and redistribute equally among our bodies. We five Sinmai on Earth are all now Oche. Poche is within us all."

They had killed Poche, as easily as wiping words off a whiteboard. I couldn't believe I had wanted to singot. If perfect understanding with others meant self-destruction, I didn't want it.

Oche's ears were twisted as he watched me. This, I realized, was what Poche realized about singot.

"Humans don't die when they share themselves with others," I said. "We become people through other people, just like you. Only, we do it a little at a time."

He asked. "Then why wouldn't you tell me? What were you scared about?"

"I felt like I had become a stranger to myself. And to other people. I thought that nobody would understand who I was, and I wouldn't understand others either. And then I would be abai forever."

His ears wiggled. "Yes!"

The Sinmai had to leave soon. They had realized that there were too few Sinmai to stay safely on Earth. Before they left, I begged the school to give them the dictionaries, and helped the children write their names in the flyleaves. Anya invited me to watch them leave. One by one they put their hands to mine and disappeared into their ship. Gouts of fire billowed beneath it as it launched, punched through the clouds, and joined the moon in the sky.

I still miss Poche, the instance of individuality that wove into Oche. By now his name must have changed again. Does the whole planet share one name? Was there ever a difference between one of him and all of them? There must have been. And there must be now. Nobody can travel to another world and return unchanged. When the crew returns home, they will greet their citizens as strangers. There will be so much for them to know about Earth. I hope their hands won't explode.

The human body limits us. We can't understand everything all at the same time. We barely understand ourselves, let alone others. But the cool thing about language is that if communication fails, you can try again. I've been talking to Anya. I told her how I thought I was asexual. And she got it! I feel embarrassed for thinking she wouldn't. Things have softened between us, started to flow onward. We're not together, not really. But we're looking in the same direction. Towards the Sinmai home world.

I've started a new career at the Institute. Being a certified friend of Sinmai helped my application jump to the top of the pile. I'll be studying Oche's language now, so I can tell him, "I know why you painted the moment you saw Earth. You were curious to know whether you were alone in the universe. And then you discovered you weren't." The Sinmai trusted that humanity was worth discovering. To live, I must too. And I can't imagine a better life than spending it with people I'll never really know, who will forever surprise me with new aspects to love, unfolding forever together.

See E.C. Fuller's story "Singot" online at
Metaphorosis.
If you liked it, leave a comment. Authors love
that!
Remember to subscribe to our e-mail updates so
you'll know when new stories are posted.

About the story

"Singot" was inspired by two things: a screenshot of a Tumblr post about how kindergarten teachers are perfect for teaching people how to be human and an NPR podcast about anthropologists believing they had discovered a new emotion. The idea that you could discover a new emotion gripped me. I had recently realized I was asexual, and I didn't like it at all. I wanted to feel something for another person; I felt messed up, but ached to share, and wanted not just to be seen, but found and spoken to. And most importantly, to be understood. Hence, singot: the wordless understanding of a person's entire life.

But if given the chance to singot, I'm not sure I would take it. When thinking back over my life I wonder, God, how I did I miss that I was asexual? I usually answer, because I was happy as I was. I love learning about the world and the people who walk on it. Why introspect when there's a zillion things to learn? And if we understand immediately, perfectly, does that mean we lose learning? I wanted to explore what we lose by understanding perfectly or imperfectly, using a strong chain of causal and emotional logic, and find an answer I could live by.

A question for the author

Q: Are titles easy or hard for you? Do you start with the title or the story?]

A: Story first, always. Usually when I begin to write a story, the title is just a descriptive tag to separate the story from all the other drafts. Titles are usually the last part I revise because they're the first thing readers read and they color the rest of the story. For example, "Singot", was nearly titled "Abai" instead. While singot appeared to be a useful solution to the character's goals, the frightening but necessary abai powers the story forward. What's more important? The push or the pull? I ultimately chose "Singot" because I felt it was the more positive title, though the end may shake that impression. Even now, I'm still not sure whether I chose the right title.

About the author

E. C. Fuller lives and works in Tulsa, OK.

ecfullersbooks.com, @birdshapedhat

Souls Like Sea Glass

Josie Smith

My entire life, I'd known three people: Pa; Ma, before she'd died giving birth to a still baby when I was four; and the ferryman who brought us our supplies and rations each month. The world I was raised in would have been an empty one for anyone else, but, for me, it was full to bursting. Our island was populated by cliffs the wind loved to beat against, a savage sea, and the stretches of sand where the wild ponies dozed. And at the edge of the island was the lighthouse built from white stone. It had risen above me from my first memory, and its light acted as a stern warning to those that sailed past our desolate part of the world.

Each evening, Pa would walk with me along our island's rocky coast, a lantern held in one hand and my fist secured in his other. He never told me what exactly we were looking for, but I found plenty to carry home in my pockets, anyway. Even at ten, I was collecting whatever I found: smooth pebbles, sea glass in countless colors, sometimes even a whole sand dollar. For me, it was full pockets, full heart. Whenever I found the rare conch shell, Pa would press it first to his ear, then to mine.

"Listen, Cora," he said. "There's no sweeter music in all the world. Even when I'm away from the sea, I can hear that tune in my dreams."

I laughed at the thought of Pa anywhere but at our lighthouse or on Hestur Island. All the time I'd know him, I'd never once seen him leave. Why would anyone want to? The island had always felt like home, like magic, to me. This place was built of it, woven from magic like a tapestry. Nothing else could explain all the wildflowers bursting from the hillsides each spring or the soft sand I'd learned to walk upon or the light always keeping watch over us.

Pa held a hand to his heart at my laughter, doing his best to act solemn despite the hidden smile twitching at his lips. "I swear it. The mainland's more than just a word. I've been to it. Even made memories there."

I wrinkled my nose. "Any that mattered?"

Pa scooped up a piece of red sea glass I'd missed, wincing at his bent back. "Nope. All the important memories are right here."

I took the sea glass from him and held it up to the sinking sun. With the last rays of light shining through it, the smooth glass burned ruby red in my hand, like a dying star. Once the sun had faded further, I tucked the glass into my pocket with everything else I'd collected.

I turned back to the lighthouse, its beam gaining brilliance against the darkening sky. "It's nearly night. Aren't we going to go back?"

Pa stepped over a large piece of driftwood and continued past me, further down the beach. "No, let's keep walking. There's something I need to show you."

I frowned and watched him go. Pa wasn't one for many rules. He had the simple ones, of course. No leaving dirty dishes, no wasting kerosene, no swimming too far out at sea. But the most important one had always been to stay inside after sunset. The island was too dangerous in the dark, Pa had insisted. Even if his own rule didn't keep him from disappearing out into the shadows every night himself.

I skipped to catch up to Pa, scattering sand as I went. "Are you finally going to let me help with the lighthouse?" I'd been begging him for years to let me do more, more, more. That it was a family role was the one thing I'd gleaned from his stories told beside the fireplace or over the dinner table. Years before I'd learned to traipse across the island's shore, Pa had taken over the lighthouse from his own pa. And from the first I'd learned of it, I'd yearned to do the same. "I can do it, you know. Everything."

Pa laughed and I crossed my arms at his amusement. "I already let you help."

"I want to do more. And I don't want to let you be alone in the dark."

"I'm never alone." He gestured back at the lighthouse. "There's always the light. But I will welcome more of your help."

We kept walking as the sky grew as black as a razorbill's wings. It was thrilling, walking along the shore after dark. My first time breaking the rule and there was a whole new facet of the island to see at night. I took it all in as I danced alongside Pa on raised toes. My hand stayed in his until he paused.

"Here." Pa handed me the lantern. I lifted it high as he coughed into his closed fist. "I did want to wait until you were older to heap so much responsibility upon you." The corner of Pa's mouth twitched, his best attempt at a smile. "But fate's done what it does best and forced my hand."

Pa might have been hesitant to hand over more responsibilities, but I didn't share his regrets. Instead, I held the lantern steady and waited beside him for whatever he wanted from me next. I would be a keeper, like him, like his pa. And I would protect this island and keep all who passed by it safe.

I smiled to myself. Maybe it was a good thing I was Pa's only living child. Someone had to be keeper after him and a short, bony daughter wouldn't likely have been anyone's first choice. But then maybe Pa would have chosen me first, anyway. He'd always said I was born of this island, built of wild winds and seagulls' cries and brine, rather than mere human flesh.

Pa was a poet, whether he was ever willing to admit it or not. The lighthouse, not me, was the usual recipient of his rhymes and uttered verses. Some days, it was 'the guide for souls lost at sea'. Others, it was 'the night's burning beacon'. I just called it the lighthouse.

Pa was less eloquent that night as he wordlessly pointed me forward. I raised an eyebrow, but didn't question him. I was too focused on the anticipation rising in me like the tide. Instead, I left Pa behind as I picked my way around a pair of tide pools and the brown boulders scattered across the higher parts of the beach. Pa's lantern lit the way forward, and I hadn't followed its light far before I paused.

There was a stranger on our island.

A pale sailor lay motionless on the sand, illuminated by the light I carried. His feet were bare and his faded blue uniform hung loosely on his bedraggled frame. The sea seemed to have spit him out onto the shore, but not before tossing him about a good bit in the waves.

Footsteps crunched in the sand behind me, and Pa's steady hand found my shoulder. I was shaking, but told myself it was because of the night's cold. Not because I'd never seen a stranger before.

Pa wasn't as bothered by the interloper on our shore. Instead, he motioned me forward. "Don't be afraid. This is what I wanted to show you tonight. Go on. Ask him his name."

I took small steps forward in the sand, tracking through the hoofprints the island's herd of wild ponies had left streaked across the beach. When I reached the unmoving sailor, I took a deep breath, swallowing all the courage I could. Eventually, I stretched out a hand and grazed his shoulder with the tips of my fingers. The sailor stirred at my slight touch, but it took another nudge from me before he lifted his head. He looked my way with eyes as empty as the night.

I bit my lip and glanced back at Pa. *Fortune follows fortitude*, he repeated often enough to be a prayer. Whether he was telling himself or me, I was never quite sure. But his words were enough to convince me then.

I stuck out my free hand toward the sailor. "Who are you? What's your name?"

"Irving." The sailor slowly rose to sit on the sand and shook my hand as his eyes lifted up, up, up to the light shining above us. "Oh. It's a lighthouse."

I held onto the lantern as Pa joined us and helped lift the sailor to his feet. "Irving, welcome to Hestur Island," he said. "The lighthouse I keep is what you saw, what brought you here. Now, if you'll follow me, I'll help you continue."

Irving pursed his lips. "That's it? Drown and move on?"

I looked between the two, curiosity singing loud to me as Pa stepped closer to the sailor. "I'm sorry. Some days the sea's kind, some days it's cruel. But you're safe here now and there's not far to go."

"My line came loose in a storm. Figured I was dead as soon as I hit the water. Never learned to swim, ya know? At least I'm not still stuck there." Irving lowered his head. "I had family back in Brighton. A wife. Two sons. There's no way to say goodbye?"

Pa tugged at the graying strands of his beard. "Afraid not. There's only going forward."

Irving let the sea wash over his feet one last time before he stepped away from it and toward Pa.

Pa clapped his shoulder and murmured, "Good man. Come, follow me and it'll all be done soon."

Pa started forward, away from the shore and inland, to where a peak rose at the island's center. I kept close to him, the way I often was, while Irving trudged along through the sand after us, his gaze focused on the ground.

"Who is that?" I whispered. "What does he mean 'drown and move on'?"

Pa took the lantern from me and held it aloft to better light the path in front of us. "This is our job, too. The light warns ships about the rocks and shallow depths. But it's also something for lost, drowned souls to anchor onto. Anyone who dies in the sea, they stay there disoriented and adrift. At least, until they find something to swim for, like moths drawn to a light."

The shore. And the light. I glanced at them both as we walked. I'd liked to imagine for years that the island was strung though with thin strands of magic. Perhaps I hadn't been so far from the truth. I had seen Irving myself. Touched him. He had been solid enough, but not

entirely human. More like an echo of a
person, standing there on the sand. And
I'd never known Pa to lie to me before.

Pa lowered his voice. "How much time
a drowned soul spends in the sea differs
for each of them. And after they wash
ashore here, I help guide them on to
whatever comes next."

"And what does come next?" The oldest
human question that even a small child
knew how to wonder about.

"No more questions, Cora." Pa took
great, heaving steps as the ground sloped.
"Just watch."

I trampled through overgrown meadow
grass, doing my best to keep up with Pa.
He led Irving and me until we were almost
to the island's center and the sea was a
sounding afterthought. Here, the ground
rose high enough that there was always
mist, even on the days the sky was clear
and bright, a seabird's paradise.

At the mist's edge, Pa shook Irving's
hand so firmly it looked final. "Sorry
you're going young. Sorry about your
family. But there oughtn't be any
hardship beyond, so go on and enjoy it."

Irving looked to the lighthouse, then to
the mist again. He shoved his shoulders
back, the same way I did whenever I was

trying to be brave for Pa. Then, he eased his way into his mist on slow steps. Its silver, reaching tendrils shifted to cocoon the sailor, blocking him from sight. I bounced on the balls of my feet and waited for him to come back out. When he didn't, I finally reached up and tapped Pa.

"Where's he going?" I said.

Pa turned from the mist and used the lantern to guide us back to the lighthouse. "Where I guide all the others to. Someplace waits for them beyond the mist, but it's not our business. We're only here to make sure the drowned souls make it." Pa frowned down at me, his thick eyebrows shoved together. "Don't waste too much time wondering about what comes after. We're still living, so it's no use asking questions meant for the dead."

"Is it just our island? How many souls?"

"Patience, Cora. A man can only answer so many questions in a night. I'm keeper on this island. Not others. I can't speak for them. And ours is an ordinary place in every aspect but one."

I jutted out my chin. Our island was not ordinary. Pa had been raised here too, so he should have known better. But he continued answering my questions, so I didn't interrupt to tell him so.

"The souls are a secret we keep so they can have peace and not be hounded by mainlanders seeking them out. And there's one to guide to the mist every week or two, but we must always be looking for them. That's the way my pa did it, too. Found the souls here, figured out what to do, taught me the same. Now, I'm teaching you."

"And the Lighthouse Board keeps the secret over on the mainland?"

Pa grunted and shook his head. "They're good for paying us and sending rations. That's about it. Think, Cora. We tell them, they decide we're not in the right state of mind to stay here, and then there's no proper keeper for the souls or the lighthouse."

I pursed my lips. Pa rarely spoke kindly of the 'meddlesome' Lighthouse Board. The lantern flickered and Pa muttered something about the oil running low.

"Keepers don't get much sleep, do they?" I said.

He chuckled and ruffled my hair. "It's a hard life, but a good one."

I made my decision then, with Pa at my side and the lighthouse gleaming ahead.

Souls, island, all of it. I'd never been born for anything else.

I was fourteen the last time I remember getting a full night's sleep and sixteen the first time I escorted a soul to the mist by myself. She had been an older woman with red hair and faint wrinkles around her eyes. Women's souls were a rare find on the shore. I had taken this one away from the lighthouse, past the moor where the ponies grazed, and right to where the mist gathered so thickly I couldn't see past it.

"Just through there," I said as I gestured the woman forward. "I don't know what happens after you step in, but good luck."

She let out a light laugh. The sound surprised me, as it didn't match the way she'd been walking earlier. Then, she had been like Atlas with the world, carrying sadness heavily on her shoulders. After thanking me for my help, the woman smiled and stepped into the mist. Then it was like she'd never been there at all, except for some slight stirring of the reaching, silver haze.

Most souls went easily, like she had. A few tried to stay, tried to fight against fate. But souls couldn't stay on the island once they had finally washed ashore. They weakened on land until they either entered the mist or faded away, losing themselves entirely. Pa had been at my side the first time a soul had argued against entering the mist right away. But from then on, I had been able to handle the more unruly souls on my own. All it usually took was a good dose of convincing, or simply sitting and talking away their fears of the unknown.

A year after I started guiding souls on my own, a particularly bad bout of pneumonia took Pa. It had been the worst winter I could remember, only made more frigid and lifeless by his passing. Since Pa hadn't drowned out among the waves, I buried him without a chance to see his soul and say a last goodbye. The dirt, the earth beneath our feet. This was home and familiar and what our souls knew. It was only those who were lost out at sea, in an unfamiliar world, that needed help and guidance.

It was Pa's death that brought me a grief as vast as the sea but also the full realization of the life I'd striven for. I became the keeper of Hestur Island, its lighthouse, and its souls. Each night, I would light Pa's old lantern and go wandering up and down the coast, collecting souls like sea glass and humming along to the tune of the crashing waves.

In my small corner of the world, I was alone. But, most of the time, I kept busy enough that the loneliness knocking on my windows couldn't find a way inside. Some nights the wind did echo too loudly and the cottage next to the lighthouse was suffocating with its emptiness. Then, I would listen to the melodies sung by my ever-growing collections of shells and mutter to myself that, even without Pa, I was not alone here on the island.

There was the herd of wild ponies that I'd tried and failed to ride as a child. They would gather on the beach at dawn each morning and both they and the sun would greet me. I always kept my distance, like Pa had taught. We were to be observers of the island's inhabitants and let nature choose its course without interfering, he said. But they were still my constant companions, along with the rough waves of the sea and the light I ensured never went out. I always had the light, and I told myself that would have to be enough.

The month after I turned twenty, I was standing on the island's one small dock when the ferryman arrived with his usual rations and supplies. He had rowed in on a dinghy from his sloop anchored out in deeper waters. On the bench beside him was a lanky, blond man. An apprentice of the ferryman's, I assumed. He was getting old, just as Pa had, and was likely to have retirement forced upon him soon.

The ferryman handed off a few crates to me, which I stacked beside my own dinghy moored to the other side of the dock. Besides the crates of supplies, the ferryman also passed over an unwanted parcel. I pursed my lips as the blond man climbed out of the boat. With unsteady legs more used to the sea than land, he clambered onto the dock. Onto my dock. Onto my island.

He stood with a hand shielding his eyes from the sun as he took in the island and the cliffs rising beyond us. The man gave a satisfied nod at the sight of it all. I ground my teeth, wanting nothing more than to chase him off the dock and out of sight. Or at the very least, shove him into the sea.

I tugged on a mask of cool politeness to help mask my sparking rage.

"Can I help you?" I said.

The man spread his feet and steadied himself as the waves swayed the dock. "I'm here to replace Douglas Timmons as the lighthouse keeper."

My eyes narrowed as I readjusted my grip on a wooden crate of rations. "Hestur Island already has a keeper. Me."

The ferryman never left his dinghy, but lifted a hand to get my attention. "The Lighthouse Board will keep on paying you, but felt more comfortable sending someone else out to help you with the upkeep of the light."

Of course, the Lighthouse Board was being meddlesome again. They and my family both considered the lighthouse to be ours, which is where the disagreements had first begun.

My face twisted. "I was raised here. I doubt some naïve recruit will be any help." I waved to the ferryman. "Take him back to the mainland, would you? I don't need another keeper, so tell the Lighthouse Board to shove that idea up—"

"Please," the man said. "The pay they offered me was more generous than any other job I could find and I have parents to support back on the mainland."

My eyes met the man's bright ones. They were the same color as the sea and I cursed myself for noticing. The ferryman said nothing, but offered me an encouraging smile. As much as I hated this, it would be a pain to fight the Lighthouse Board. Pa had never had any success with that while he'd been alive. It was difficult to argue against the orders of those that paid me and sent my rations. Coexist, it was.

My sigh was perhaps more dramatic than necessary. "Just promise me you won't be a hindrance."

The young man straightened the old, weathered cap he wore and stretched out a hand. Never mind that I didn't exactly have a free one to offer him. "I promise I'm only here to make your job easier, ma'am. I'm Morgan Fisk."

I repositioned the crate to rest on my hip and begrudgingly shook his hand. After that, I stepped aside and let him off the dock. Morgan grabbed a crate of his own to carry before stepping onto my island.

Back at the lighthouse, once the ferryman had sailed off, I hoisted a can of kerosene into Morgan's arms. He grunted at its heft and gripped its handle in a tight fist.

"Run that up to the top," I said. "I'll unpack the rest of these crates."

Morgan turned and entered through the lighthouse door, staggering under the kerosene's weight. So far, the lone tolerable thing about him had been his saving me time by helping to carry crates from the dock. Or the way I could make him climb all the stairs with the kerosene instead of doing it myself. If Morgan was going to remain here, he might as well do the less pleasurable parts of the job.

Dinner that night was near silent. I alternated between glaring at my tablemate and swallowing under-seasoned stew. Despite all my requests, the ferryman never arrived with nearly as many spices as I preferred to cook with.

Morgan chuckled as he scraped his bowl clean with a tarnished spoon. He'd left his nervous politeness behind on the dock. "I'm the only other person for miles.

If you insist on hating me, it's going to be a very lonely life."

"I've done lonely. It doesn't bother me." I stared at the chair Morgan occupied. Not long ago, Pa had sat there filling the room with light and life. Some part of me had wanted the chair in use again, but not by somebody else.

Morgan tapped his fingers against the wooden table. "I didn't say you would be the only lonely one."

Not willing to have this conversation, I rose and hurried my used dishes over to the sink. Years of following Pa's rules hadn't been forgotten, and so I washed my bowl and spoon while standing with my back to Morgan.

The silence I'd come to know suddenly felt strange with someone else in the room. I didn't face Morgan again until I'd wiped my dishes dry and placed them in the cupboard above.

"I don't hate you," I said. "I just wish you weren't here."

His brows furrowed. "And there's supposed to be a whole lot of difference in that?"

"Make yourself useful on the island. Then maybe I'll change my mind."

I shrugged on a long woolen coat and grabbed Pa's old lantern. Morgan placed his own dishes in the sink before joining me at the door.

I shook my head. "Stay here and make sure the light keeps shining."

"Where are you going, then?"

"I'm going to look for..." The souls were certainly not Morgan's secret to learn so soon. The Lord alone knew whether he would be a danger to them or could even properly keep a secret. "The lighthouse keeps ships clear of the rocky waters here, but the far side of the island can sometimes be a magnet for wrecks. I walk that part each night to make sure there's no trouble."

Morgan nodded, fully accepting the way I'd masked the truth of this place. "Stay safe," he said. "I'll keep everything here in working order."

"Don't wait up." I opened the cottage door and stepped through it. "I might be gone a while."

The night was cold, and I found no souls on the shore. When I was done wandering the coast, I yanked my coat tighter around myself and let the lighthouse's beam pull me back home. I trudged back up to the cottage, already thinking about the fire I'd light. But when I was nearly at the door, a candle flickering in the window made me pause. Morgan must have put it there while I was gone.

I entered the cottage and yanked the door shut behind me, sealing out the frigid wind that had battered me the whole time I'd been gone. Morgan sat in an armchair, half-asleep and trying to read by a single lamp.

I hung my coat on a peg by the door. "Why the candle? We don't need one in the window and we can't waste light like that."

"I thought it might be a good signal." Morgan closed his book and set it on a side table. "If you're going to be out walking after dark often, then I'll keep it lit if I'm here and awake. That way you'll know whether to be quiet or not. Or if you need to look for me."

I laughed. "Are you a light sleeper?"

Morgan nodded.

"You won't stay that way."

But his candle in the window did end up becoming a habit of ours. A silent message saying, *I'm here, I'm home, I'm waiting.* And while I'd first let him do it because it wasn't worth the fight, I eventually grew to look forward to seeing it. I'd come home from the shore each night and there it was; a little lighthouse of our own gleaming against the windowpane. Meanwhile, the rare dark window meant I was alone for the night. I learned to despise the sight of it.

After so many days of silence, it took me time to adjust to the sudden influx of sound and song the new keeper had brought with him. There was someone else on the island and it wasn't Pa. But Morgan took to island life like a bird to flight, never complaining of the long hours nor the lighthouse's many chores. The constant roar of the sea in the distance was now often punctuated by Morgan's voice. He liked to talk and enjoyed singing even more. Old folk songs, ballads, shanties. He would utter them all while he worked.

I'd be at the lighthouse's peak, sweeping the dust and sand from the floor or clearing the grime from the windows when Morgan would hunt me down. Years spent nigh on alone had made me comfortable with my own company, but the mainlander abhorred the silence and repeated every thought that passed through his head.

While we worked on repainting the cottage a bright, pure white, Morgan recounted all his summers spent painting fences and buildings on the farm where he'd been raised.

"No wonder your paintwork looks so good," I said once he'd finished. My half of the cottage was functionally white, but Morgan's was all broad, smooth strokes and no streaks. His height made the difference, I told myself.

"Years of practice." Morgan gestured upward. "Like you with that towering lighthouse."

I dropped my paintbrush and wiped paint from my fingers. "Good, I'll let you finish painting the entire cottage then."

At his protests, I laughed and picked up the brush again. Morgan's hands weren't so steady and sure the following days as I showed him how to trim wicks and refill the lamp's oil and all the other daily tasks. He'd been here long enough and been enough of a help that I didn't mind teaching him more. Or answering his countless questions about the lighthouse and myself.

"And you've lived here your whole life?"

"Yep."

"Don't you want to visit the mainland? At least once?"

"Nope."

"What's your favorite part of the island?"

I paused, for the first time having to think about how to answer one of Morgan's questions. My attention left his hands, the ones I'd been guiding through trimming the wick. Instead, I met his eyes.

The souls. The words nearly flew from my lips, but I pressed them together to shut in any sound.

"The wild ponies," I said instead.

It was those same wild ponies that stole Morgan away from me weeks later. I roused right as dawn was breaking over the shore, ready to dampen the lighthouse's beam. But the cottage was empty, and when I called for Morgan to help, there was no answer.

Finding him again didn't take much time. I checked the lighthouse for Morgan as soon as I stepped from the cottage and sealed the door shut behind me. But it was on the shore that I found him, the echo of his voice carried my way by the wind.

The herd of wild ponies was there on the stretch of sand like they were every morning. Morgan knelt among them, right next to a mare lying on her side. My silent steps hurried along as I made my way through the sand. I reached Morgan and knelt beside him on the ground the lowering tide had left damp.

Wheeling birds called overhead, their cries nearly as shrill as the whinny the mare released. Morgan spoke to her, calm and quiet, slower than I'd ever heard him before. I remained still beside him, there if he needed the help but otherwise a motionless observer.

It was second nature observing, like Pa had taught. But for the first time, I went against it. Morgan was already fighting for this foal to live. I found myself desiring the same for his sake. Together, we urged the mare on as I knelt beside him.

Many days, with the souls, death was all I saw. I grew tired of witnessing it sometimes. Now, I sat back on my heels and tucked away a loose strand of hair. Nature could choose its own course, its decided deaths, another day. Today, I wanted this foal to live.

I scuttled backward a few minutes later as Morgan lunged for the foal who'd finally emerged from the panting mare. With hands that refused to shake, he eased the foal's head free and cleared its nostrils. The mare heaved to her feet and nickered at her baby. And as she licked him clean, the foal took his first breath of sea air.

I gasped with joy and tugged at Morgan's arm. "He's breathing. Will he be alright?"

He leaned back on his heels and nodded. "Should be. But I want to stay awhile to make sure mare and foal are both steady."

I stared at Morgan while he watched the ponies keenly. He knelt in the sand with dirty hands and not a single care other than the ponies', the island's, wellbeing. And it felt good to see something breathe and live, not be guided to the mist and sent away. There was more life on the island now, with Morgan's help. Perhaps it hadn't been such a cruel fate the day he had stepped onto my dock. Perhaps he would be good for the island. Every part of it.

"How did you know what to do?" I said. "Or even to come down to the herd at all?"

Morgan stepped a few paces away to wash his hands off in the saltwater. His mouth quirked and he smiled back at me. "Grew up on a farm, remember? I've delivered countless foals. I heard the mare's whinnies when I woke this morning and rushed down to help." He knelt beside me again. "Want to name the foal?"

I shook my head. "They're the island's. Not ours."

Morgan leaned over and kissed my cheek, nearly making me jump. "Good point. Thank you for your help."

I'd expected to hate his touch. But I hadn't. Not at all.

Inching closer together, we watched at the edge of the herd in silence as the foal took his first steps on long, uncertain legs. He learned to walk on that shore, just as I had years ago. From his smile and straight back, I could see that Morgan took pride in watching the foal walk; the foal he had acted to save and protect.

At that moment, I decided. Finally, I would trust him with the island's most precious secret, its shipwrecked souls. That night, I took Morgan with me from the cottage and used the lantern to light our way. Down at the beach, I stayed back and ushered him on ahead toward the one soul we found. Better to show him, rather than try to explain first. Morgan was cautious, curious, as he stepped closer to the soul. I recognized those tentative steps. They were the same ones I'd taken as a child when Pa had first shown me a soul.

We walked the man from the shore to the mist, both the lighthouse and my lantern illuminating the final steps he took. Morgan stood behind me as I directed the soul into the mist. He was silent the whole way back to the cottage, an irregularity for Morgan. He didn't speak again, and only to ask a few questions, until we were seated at the kitchen table, each with a tin cup of coffee. Bitter stuff, but a necessity for ever-tired lighthouse keepers.

Morgan's voice was unsteady, quizzical, and he kept looking down at his coffee rather than meet my eyes. Perhaps it had all been easier for a young girl to accept. So, I showed him this side of the island slowly, steadily, again and again. Morgan would walk the shore each night with me and, in the three weeks that followed, we guided four more souls to the mist. With each one, Morgan spoke more, touched their hands, and lost the hesitant look in his eyes. And eventually, it must have seemed less like a strange dream and more like the reality we shared. Funny how sometimes the two collided.

After the fourth soul, we sat in the kitchen with coffee again, something that had become habit by then.

"The souls, they really do come, don't they?" Morgan muttered, more to himself than me.

I crossed my legs and rested my hands on the table. I'd give him time for all this. As much as he needed. As many souls as it took.

Finally, Morgan looked up at me. "I hope that man can find peace," he said. His mind, like mine, must still have been focused on the soul we'd said goodbye to. It had been more hesitant than usual to leave this place.

"They do in the mist," I said. "I think." I swallowed some of my coffee. Pa and the souls themselves had never given me a reason to believe otherwise.

Morgan nodded and, while we sat there, I placed my hand on top of his so they both rested atop the worn table. The nearby candle in the window didn't give off much light, but it was enough to see by. Smiling, Morgan curled his calloused fingers around mine and we stayed that way until long after our coffee was finished. After that night, it was like he'd finally decided his role for himself, as he didn't hesitate with the souls any longer.

We spent our days and nights working at the lighthouse and guiding souls. Occasionally hand-in-hand, but always together. Daylight hours were for climbing up and down countless stairs and doing the necessary chores. After stars were threaded into the sky's dark tapestry each night, we walked the beach, sharing a lantern between us. The lighthouse's bright, burning beam never flickered or went out, nor did our candle in the window. And somewhere in between all that, we found time to splash each other in the surf and learned to share kisses that tasted of salt and sea air.

Our world was a steady one of light and life and long, working days. The lighthouse kept me strong and Morgan kept my heart light. We found we were good at forming our own small family. Each for the other, we were solid ground and familiar, comforting sea breeze and a shining light in the dark.

One night, like always, Morgan and I were walking along the shore, searching for souls. We had found none so far and were debating returning to the cottage when cries for help caught my attention. I lifted my head and tugged on Morgan's arm. At my pointing, we both fixed our gaze on the ship foundering out on the rocks. Even with the light's warning, it had strayed too close to the shore. The rough waves and sharp rocks had met their prey wholeheartedly, leaving the ship in poor, wrecked shape.

After we sighted the ship, Morgan and I both hurried to our lone dinghy moored to the dock. Each of us with an oar in hand, we rowed out past breaking waves to the ship. I spent so much time guiding drowned souls that sometimes it felt like I overlooked the other part of my job: keeping living souls from drowning in the first place. I tightened my grip on the oar and leaned forward to row a little faster.

When we reached the ship, it had become stuck between two large rocks jutting out from the sea. The ship's surviving occupants had all gathered on the highest, least water-logged point. With both oars, Morgan and I kept the dinghy steady enough to maneuver around rocks and reach the soaking men.

"We're from the lighthouse," I called to them, hoping they could hear me above the wind. "We're here to take you back to shore."

Morgan surveyed the terrified faces of the men. "It's going to be tight, but I think one trip will make it."

I nodded. I turned away from Morgan as we tried to get the dinghy as close to the men as we could. Rather than risk our own dinghy being beaten against the ship by the waves, we kept it a few paces away. The men who were able to swim made it over and we hauled them aboard.

"Keep the dinghy nearby," I told Morgan before diving into the water.

I swam for the rest of the men, dragging each back to the dinghy and keeping their heads above the waves. The sea was cold and rough, but I'd grown up swimming in it. Eventually, I made it to the dinghy with the last of the ship's survivors. We left the wreck behind as I took my oar back and began paddling again.

The dinghy was heavier and more difficult to maneuver, but we made progress as Morgan and I continued to take strokes through the seawater. I groaned from the effort rowing took as we made it to the first of the breaking waves. Rather than aim for the dock, we headed for the expanse of shore, just trying to get everyone back to land.

One of the men crammed to the side was thrown over the dinghy's edge as a particularly rough wave knocked the boat. I cursed as I watched him go. Just when I'd been starting to dry off.

Before I could dive in after the man, Morgan had pulled off his own jacket and jumped into the sea. "You've already had your turn," he called to me. "Just get those men back to shore. I'll get this one."

I smiled my thanks. I was already shivering, so it was a blessing not having to dive back into the water.

"Take that oar and help me," I said, gesturing to one of the less pale-looking men.

Another round of hard rowing brought the dinghy close to shore. As it ground against the sandy bottom, I jumped out. Others followed and we pulled the dinghy fully onto dry land where it would be safe from the rising tide.

I shoved back a strand of dripping hair and turned to the sea, expecting to see Morgan swimming back right behind me. But even with no lantern, I couldn't see any man adrift in the sea. I ran to the edge of the waves and scanned the dark sea through narrowed eyes. Even calling Morgan's name brought no answer.

With no sign of him, I ran back into the sea itself. I swam out to where I'd seen him last and dove down, searching for him countless times. I looked for him among the waves until I had no breath left. Both Morgan and the man he had gone to rescue were gone, stolen away by the sea.

I returned to the shore once I was gasping for breath and my arms were refusing to take another stroke. Wordlessly, I led the rescued sailors back to the cottage. They sat gathered in front of the fireplace and wrapped in every blanket and towel I could find. We made the food and water stretch, and after another five days, the ferryman arrived for the month. When he left, he took the sailors with him and I was alone again with only the candle burning in the window.

I lit it again, night after night, while the cruel sea sang its song outside my dark, empty home. My work stayed the same, night and day, but this time there was no hand in mine and no light in my life.

Summer eventually left and took the last of its blazing warmth with it.

Day after day passed, each filled with pacing and waiting and walking the shore for hours. Many nights, I debated aloud with myself in my empty cottage. My drowned love would return to me, to my shore. And it had quickly occurred to me that though I would guide him into the mist, there was nothing keeping me from following him in. Except that I had a duty here, a role to fulfill. There was no leaving this island so easily.

But there would be peace in the mist, with Morgan, and I wouldn't be keeping the souls and the lighthouse alone anymore. *This island doesn't need to remain your charge*, a voice would sometimes repeat in my head. But that voice was not me, no matter how many times I tried to convince myself that it was.

It took time, too much time, but eventually, the night I'd been waiting for arrived. I had been walking barefoot through the sand with my lantern held aloft while the wind whipped my hair about. Then there he was, lying on his side in front of me with ocean foam stuck in his hair. Like an apology from the sea, saying, *Here, look, I gave him back to you.*

I set my lantern down and ran to him. Tears dripped from my face and mixed with the saltwater at my feet.

"Morgan." I wiped away tears with the back of my rough hand. "You came home."

He stood, appearing as solid as the other souls had and sharing their lost, empty eyes too. But as his gaze focused on me, Morgan's lost look faded in a way that had never happened with the others. His footsteps were silent as he closed the last bit of distance between us.

He, his soul, pressed his lips to mine and while there was no longer any warmth there, he still tasted of salt and summer.

Morgan was home, for a moment, for as long as I could have him. He'd either enter the mist and be lost to me then, or he would stay and fade away until there wasn't a whisper of him left on the island. This was all that we had. A quick, final goodbye. It was more than I'd had with Pa, though, and I was grateful for it.

Morgan and I walked silently back to the cottage together. My lantern's light kept many of the shadows away, but some forced their way between us anyway. We strode slowly together, Morgan's hand gripping mine so tightly it seemed he wouldn't ever let go again.

He smiled when he first glimpsed the candle shining in the window. "You kept the light on for me."

I squeezed his hand and leaned my head against his shoulder. "Always." Another stray tear fell. "Morgan, what happened?"

He kissed the top of my head. "The man who fell out of the dinghy. He was too scared and wouldn't stop fighting against me. And the waves were strong. Eventually, we both grew too exhausted, I suppose. I'm just glad you're alright."

I turned to face him. Not without him, I wasn't. Not fully. For a moment, I thought again about walking into the mist with Morgan. I wouldn't be facing the dark and the loneliness anymore that way. But that idea left me as I cast my gaze out over the savage, singing sea and the moor where the wild ponies grazed and the lighthouse shining above it all. This island, these souls, needed me. I'd taken it all on years ago, chose it again every day, and I couldn't abandon it all now. Not even for Morgan. But I couldn't let him go into the mist thinking I wouldn't be alright.

I surveyed Morgan as the sea breeze whipped around my loose strands of hair. "Thank you for the time you gave me. But don't worry about me now. I'll be fine. I promise."

I'd done lonely before. Surely, I could do lonely again.

Morgan's eyes shone as bright as the light overhead. "I don't know if I can wait... there. The mist. But I'll try. If I can."

We exchanged no more words, only held onto each other tightly as we crossed the dark, windswept island. Our pace was slow but still we reached the end of us. In the distance, the sea serenaded us as we approached where the mist rested up upon the hillside.

"I'll keep the candle in the window," I said. "Stay safe wherever you go."

"I'd stay right here if I could choose."

I nodded right before Morgan leaned down to kiss me. He murmured his final goodbye so quietly I almost missed it. Morgan walked into the mist with his head lifted. He strode alone while I stood back, wiping tears from my face. And when he was gone, I stared after him into the mist, seeing nothing more than silver and light.

Though he'd gone, Morgan stayed with me in ways I hadn't expected. I was reminded of him each time I saw the black foal he'd helped deliver. The foal splashed through the surf on the shore each morning, growing ever stronger and taller. Soon he wouldn't need his mama anymore and would be mating himself. And every day, I made two cups of coffee, one for Morgan and one for me. It was a habit that wouldn't die. One I couldn't bring myself to let fade away.

The island refused to go back to its original silence. While I worked, I hummed to myself all the old folk songs Morgan had brought over from the mainland. He'd taught me many while he'd been here. Some nights by the sea, I swore I could still hear his voice on the wind.

His leaving had shattered me, but I slowly stitched the scraps of myself back together. I'd said my goodbye, decided to stay, and took each day as it came, one breath at a time. Eventually, the breathing got easier. And a few weeks later, just when I was getting used to the empty cottage, I discovered Morgan had left one last piece of himself on the island. One last gift from the dead to the living, set to arrive when the island became spring's canvas and wildflowers covered the hills again.

It was a girl I gave birth to one morning, right when the sun was dawning on the horizon. I'd never felt so grateful, knowing I was past the woes of pregnancy. I'd climbed a lot of stairs and managed as best I could with the lighthouse. For several weeks, I'd debated having another keeper sent out to help. But Morgan had been a stroke of fortune. I might not be that lucky again. No, I trusted only myself with the souls.

I smiled down at the small girl I held in my arms. Well, perhaps there was one more here I would trust with the souls and the island. But for now, she rested, her hands curled into fists and her eyes closed. From her first cry, she had chased away all the shadows left behind after Morgan's death. My own small sun. My light.

I clutched my daughter tighter as the slope I walked on steepened and meandered further uphill. She was wrapped in the gray blanket I'd knitted for her, and dozed as I crossed the island. It wasn't a far walk, but with the baby, I traveled slowly and kept stopping to pick wildflowers. White, yellow, blue. I added them all to the bouquets I gathered as I wove my way along the island's sloping side.

Further inland, I reached the place where I'd buried Pa. A wooden cross I'd made with my own hands from driftwood marked the place. A second was now rooted in the dirt beside the first, wind-battered one.

I set down the twin wildflower bouquets, each placed against a driftwood cross. With my daughter secured in my arms, I stood between the crosses with the mist at my back and the sea humming its wild song ahead.

"Ellen," I murmured, at last finding a name as my gaze came to rest on the lighthouse. Morgan's daughter with my mother's name. It was one way I could think to further merge our families, to make a place for both of us on the island.

"Ellen, this is all in your blood." I closed my eyes and let the sun kiss my face. "I hope one day you'll be a fine keeper."

Ellen grew like I had, raised under the sun and the stars and the lighthouse's shining beam. She had Morgan's eyes, a blue as pure as the sea. And it was the sea's shore she ran along so often, chasing seagulls and echoing their cries.

"Show me your pockets," was what I repeated nearly every day as I stood with a hand against the door, refusing to let Ellen go out until she obeyed. And often I caught the bread or rolls she'd been sneaking out to feed the birds on the beach.

"Please," she'd plead. "They're hungry."

"They already have food to eat. We need the bread."

Occasionally, I'd let Ellen feed the birds what she snuck from the dinner table. But with supplies and rations lasting us just until the ferryman next came, I couldn't allow it to become a daily habit.

Ellen's crooked smile was near-constant. I thought I'd been raised half-feral, but it was a fight to get the girl inside at all. She refused to wear shoes most of the time and insisted on keeping her hair shorn so it wouldn't get in the way. Every spring, she'd weave dozens of wildflower crowns and try to get the wild ponies to wear them. Lord knows the child would have been happier if I'd locked her out of the cottage and sent her to live with the herd.

Like Morgan, she adored music and songs. She collected them, like I had done with whatever I'd found on the beach when I was young. I taught Ellen all the songs I knew and the ones I'd learned from Morgan. The ferryman gave her others and the rest she stole from the island's songbirds or made up on her own.

The first soul she met, she chose to sing to. When I first brought her to the beach after dark, Ellen was younger than I'd been. But I wanted her to have the chance to grow with the souls, to know them before she was ever tasked with their care and guidance.

Ever fearless, she'd gone right up to the drowned woman. With her head cocked and one hand on her hip, Ellen had said, "What's your name?"

"Lillian."

"I'm Ellen." She jabbed a finger toward where I stood holding a lantern. "That's Ma. This is Hestur Island."

After gently explaining to the two how the soul had come to be here and what came next, I led Lillian to the mist. Ellen had been humming while we walked, and after a few minutes, Lillian turned to her.

"Will you sing louder?" She stepped around long blades of grass fluttering in the wind. "Music's always been a comfort to me."

Ellen smiled her consent and raised her voice. After that, the lilt of her song often cut through the dark. I tried to insist on Ellen staying at the cottage to sleep, but once she knew about the souls, there was no fighting her. She'd join me and bring her song with her, more often than not. The souls loved it. They loved her.

A thousand sunsets came and went. My daughter took to carrying kerosene herself. Her eyes grew bright, her legs grew strong, and her hands grew steady and sure. Morgan's child, my child, and I loved her more each time the sun rose. We guided souls together, she and I, side by side, until the night I stumbled.

I'd slipped on a stone slick from rain. It went clattering down the hill and I scraped my knees, landing on them rather than my hands. My best attempt at keeping the lantern's glass from shattering.

"Ma!" Ellen was at my side the moment the stone had gone clattering. She was stronger than me by then, taller too, and it was no trouble for her to pull me back up. The soul we'd been guiding stood nearby, watching everything without a word.

"Sorry," I said, coughing into my fist. After that, it took me a minute to get my breath back.

Ellen furrowed her brows as she looked me over. "Why don't you wait here? I'll finish the walk to the mist while you rest and then I'll be back."

I wouldn't have accepted her offer if my legs hadn't been hurting from the fall. Ellen left with the lantern and the soul. I found a boulder and crossed my legs to rest atop it. My daughter's first time escorting a soul to the mist and I hadn't even planned for it.

"I'm sorry," I repeated to her as we traveled back to the cottage later. "I should still be able to shoulder the task."

"Ma, there's no need to be Atlas. I've wanted this for years."

I turned away so she wouldn't see the tears that fell. I'd repeated the same thing to Pa many times.

"I'm afraid it's the bloodline," I said. "Pa had weak lungs and a bad back. It seems I might be afflicted too."

"Maybe it's duty, not illness, that's inherited." Ellen twisted her head and shot me that crooked grin. "Lighthouse keeper isn't an easy life. Fifty years of that, anyone would be the same."

Her words and the realization they'd brought silenced me until we made it back to the lighthouse.

"I don't regret it, you know," I said.

Ellen helped me out of my coat before pulling me close. "I never thought you did. Don't think I will either."

"You could go to the mainland. Live there awhile. The Lighthouse Board can send another keeper."

Ellen stepped back and shook her head. "No, it's our island. Our lighthouse. And we're the ones to guide the souls."

I started brewing coffee for two, the way I had for years. "I don't want to leave you here alone."

"I won't be alone. Not on this island." Ellen took the tin cup I offered her. "Besides, I had you for years longer than my pa did." She took a long sip. "I hope he's waiting, like he said he would."

I gave her a thin smile. "Me too."

We sat finishing our coffee as a candle flickered in the window, keeping the dark at bay.

I stayed with Ellen until the first snow of that year. Life had caught up to me quicker than I'd ever expected. I was nearly as pale as the snow itself and had trouble making it to the top of the lighthouse anymore. In the end, it had been Ellen's urging that convinced me. Go to the mist while I could still walk there and decide my fate for myself. After a lifetime of walking to the mist's edge, it almost felt right to walk in myself rather than being lowered down into the dirt.

My island and its souls were being left to the best possible hands. I'd seen to it myself. And maybe, just maybe, my old love would be on the other side of it all.

I left Ellen my lantern, my coat, and my love. She guided me like she would have any old soul, somehow not shedding a tear once.

"I love you, Ma," she said simply, like it was the clearest of facts.

I put my arms around her and didn't let go for a long, long time. My daughter, my girl, with eyes like the sea and a voice to rival its own tune.

"You are my light." I kissed the top of her head. "And you will be an excellent keeper. This island, these souls, are blessed to have you here."

It was Ellen who broke away first. She led me the last few steps, the same way we'd done for so many other souls. And then I entered the mist. It was peace and it was light and it was a joy fluttering in my heart like a seabird. It was a joy to rival what I'd known and found all those years on the island. A joy that embalmed me until I forgot all else.

Each morning, dawn rises on Hestur Island, painting over the stars with its fragile, pastel shades as the sea sings on below. In the place where the souls wash ashore at night, a herd of wild ponies gathers to watch as a new day is born. On the herd's edge, two bays with coats wet from sea spray stand and nuzzle each other.

The woman who guides the souls and keeps the lighthouse knows the herd well. She was raised with them, among them, nearly a wild pony herself in her youth. She doesn't recognize the two newcomers and notices them the first morning they appear. It's as if the sea sent the pair of bays itself, the way they appeared out of nowhere, out of the night.

The woman smiles to herself and goes back to her work. Soon, the two ponies become as much a part of the island as the mist and the shore and the cliffs. Like they were there from its very formation when it rose up out of the sea. Day after day, the island persists and so do they.

On the shore each morning, the two ponies stand, pressed close together as light appears on the horizon, right in the place where the sky meets the sea.

See Josie Smith's story "Souls Like Sea Glass" online at Metaphorosis.
If you liked it, leave a comment. Authors love that!
Remember to subscribe to our e-mail updates so you'll know when new stories are posted.

About the story

I'm a shameless Pinterest addict and keep an entire folder full of distinctive images that inspire me for one reason or another. One night while scrolling through the app, I came across an image of a woman holding a lantern aloft while standing on a windswept shore. Something in my mind whispered that she was searching for souls and I latched onto the idea.

I'd been taking a creative writing class for fun that semester and needed to turn in a short story. I love writing but tend to stick to poetry and novels so short stories were a new challenge for me. This idea worked perfectly for the length I needed to turn in and I had so much fun writing it. Not caring about making a first draft perfect, I had thrown in everything I love and always try to include in my writing: a wild, inspiring natural setting, tenacious girls, and hints of history and folklore woven throughout.

I'd never intended to take the story any further than my class, but after turning in my final, polished draft for the semester, I decided to submit it to a few places and just see what would happen. Then, with some more polish and rewriting, it found a home! I'm so excited to see my story in print and hope you enjoy reading it nearly as much as I enjoyed writing it.

A question for the author

Q: What is your favourite short story?

A: "Mother Carey's Table" by J. Anderson Coats. From the first paragraph, the voice wowed me, and the mix of fables, folklore, and history captured my attention. That blend is right where I try to place my own stories, so it was so fun to read. I loved the story, and the rest of the anthology, so much that I bought my own copy as soon as I finished reading the library's edition.

About the author

When not traveling, Josie Smith splits her time between Ohio and Alabama, where she is currently earning a dual degree in English and Spanish. She loves seeing new places, experiencing new things, and taking pictures of both the former. When not trying to catch up on homework, she interns for a literary agent and writes stories set in the place where magic and history intersect.

@_josiesmith

Free Hugs

Jennifer Shelby

Beware: Hugbot ahead, warned a scrawl of white paint across a brick wall. Cyndl paused in her journey through the dead city and stared at the words while a complicated blend of grief and hope blossomed inside of her.

She defied the graffiti and kept moving until the alley opened into a treed square. The Hugbot gleamed in the center, caught in a halo of sunlight and memory. Its body was vaguely humanoid: a metal torso with arms, a short vertical indentation to suggest legs, and tracks instead of feet. Its head was a silver egg with eyes and a mouth. Cyndl had heard that the original prototypes had been sleek, sophisticated, and more human-like, only to be scrapped when people used them for something more than innocent hugging.

The foam latex along the bot's inner arms, chest, and neck, once offering a pillowed embrace, now hung in ragged ribbons. Its pressure sensors would still be in good shape; the engineers had taken special care with those to prevent crushed customers and their associated lawsuits.

A thick chain around its left track tethered the robot to a link hammered into the concrete. A ring around this anchor had been grooved into the cement by the bot's desperate, hopeless circling. Cyndl curled her lip in disgust. "That kind of cruelty is never necessary," she muttered to herself.

The bot's ocular receptors were dark, and a dusty cobweb drifted lazily over the mesh speaker that was its mouth. Cyndl wiped it away, her hand lingering on the familiar oval of the metal face. A whisper of tears prickled at her eyes.

Someone had tied a filthy sheet around the neck of the bot, covering the solar panel. This had likely been meant as a kindness; a temporary means to keep the bot powered down. The rotten fabric fell apart under Cyndl's fingers as she untied it, and the sheet whooshed to the ground in a plume of disintegrated fibres.

The solar matrix beneath the sheet appeared to be in good condition. 'No wonder these things survived the Climate Wars,' Cyndl thought.

She knelt to detach the chain from the Hugbot's foot track. The links were strong, but she had a hacksaw in the patched pack that never left her side. She pushed dirty strands of silvered hair behind her sunburnt, peeling ear, set her jaw, and began to work.

Sweat soaked through her shirt by the time she'd finished and kicked the chain away. The bot had yet to wake up. It usually took a few hours for the solar batteries to charge.

Six-year-old Cyndl forced herself to walk. Her cheeks burned with the salt of dried tears. The wind whipping over the city stung her face, but if she turned away, she'd see the tower, and she did not want to see the tower.

Cyndl wasn't supposed to be alone in the ravaged world. She was supposed to be in the digital realm with the Technicians who'd built the tower, but they had flopped and soiled themselves as the electricity uploaded them to the realms. Her fear had overpowered her faith and she'd pulled out her upload cable.

Cyndl collapsed into a puddle, taking long drinks that tasted of earth and filled her mouth with silt. A glint of metal shifted in the space between her and the edges of the city, a reflected light that drew closer until a machine materialized.

The robot's shadow fell over her and it lifted her with gentle arms, cradling her body as it carried her away from the tower. She slipped in and out of consciousness. Each time she awoke anew, the bot's lights blinked. "Would you like a hug?" it asked her.

Cyndl shook her head to ground herself in the present. The Hugbot would be charged soon. She pulled a crab apple from an overgrown ornamental and sat on the ledge of a dry fountain, taking a bite and watching the city for movement. The crab apple tasted tart, but it was wet and fresh, and she relished the treat.

Wild animals had claimed the rotting city, birds flying from broken windows and raccoons skulking through open doorways. The old Tech Cults had been the last hangers-on to sedentary lifestyles, but people still marked their travels by these ruined cities. A Technician tower loomed at the edge of the western skyline. There was a tower for every dead city, but Cyndl didn't like to acknowledge them.

The first lights flickered on the bot's control panel. It opened its eyes and turned its head to her. "Would you like a hug?"

Cyndl closed her eyes for a moment, overcome by the emotional weight of the familiar, tinny voice. "Hey, Hugbot."

"I am Unit 2201. I was created to provide safe physical contact." The bot projected a hologram of a nondescript individual in a suit into the air between them. Cyndl had dubbed this person Hugbob when she was little. "Here at Lovelace Robotics, we know how hard it is to refrain from hugging your loved ones as we do our duty to defeat the virus. That is why Lovelace Robotics created the Safe Family Avatar. Now you can send Grandma what she really wants for her birthday: a hug from her grandchildren."

In the grainy hologram, an elderly woman wept into the robot's neck as it embraced her. "The Safe Family Avatar's upper body is made of soft, padded latex for the feel of a real hug. Using our patent-pending, non-invasive technology, our Safe Family Avatars scan the levels of oxytocin, the human happiness hormone, in your hug recipient's bloodstream. This enables us to ensure the optimal hormone levels for best mental health benefits have been achieved. Following each embrace, the Safe Family Avatar engages Disinfect Protocol, designed to destroy any germs that may have been transferred during physical contact."

The hologram shut down. "Free hugs," said the bot.

Tears tracked down Cyndl's cheeks, but a small smile waited on her lips. "The Hugbot who raised me played that hologram for me whenever I had nightmares." She cocked her head. "They found me after I escaped from the Tech Cults and they taught me how to survive. And, of course, I hugged them whenever their programming told them they needed one."

The Hugbot didn't say anything and Cyndl giggled nervously. "Sorry if I'm talking too much. It's been a while since I've had a Hugbot to talk to." She gave an awkward shrug. "I'm on my own a lot. I've tried to join traveling groups, but I never last long. The nightmares come back." She considered the crab apple core in her hand. Its pink flesh had oxidized to a rusty brown.

"Travelers do not like hugs," said the Hugbot.

"No." She tossed the core onto the ground.

"People are afraid of Unit 2201," said the Hugbot.

"That's not your fault." Cyndl gestured in the direction of the tower. "After the Tech Cults, people got superstitious of machines. You bots are the black cats of the modern world."

"Safe Family Avatars are not cats," said the Hugbot.

"It means they think crossing your path brings bad luck." Cyndl eyed the bot to gauge its reaction, but the robot did nothing. "It's not your fault that your programming tortures you when you have no one to hug, either. Your programmers just wanted you to work hard; they didn't expect this." She held up an end of the chain she'd cut away from its track.

"Would you like a hug?" asked the Hugbot.

"How long has it been since someone hugged you?" asked Cyndl.

"Thirty-two years, eight months, seven days."

Cyndl winced. "That's a long time, Hugbot. When your Disinfectant Protocol goes off after that long without use, it's probably going to kill you. I've seen it happen a few times with other Hugbots. But if it doesn't..." Cyndl tried to push down a surge of hope with a gulping breath. "We could travel together. I lost my Hugbot a long time ago."

A sob burst out of Cyndl as she lunged the wagon forward, stepping into the shadow of a Technician tower for the first time since she'd failed to upload. The Hugbot in the wagon listed severely to the right, its bottom half and track assembly melted into a blob of silvery metals. "FREE HUGS FREE HUGS FREE HUGS!"

Tiny lights inside the tower winked red and green; it still had power. An upload cable waited inside. Cyndl swallowed hard, her hand unwilling to reach out and grab the thing. The robot's voice burst through the memory that threatened to surface. "HUGS FREE FREE." And then the cord was in her hand and she was wrapping the Hugbot's metal fingers around it.

"Once I turn the power on, the current will fry your circuits. It'll be just like the Hugbot we saw that got hit by lightning. You'll be dead."

"FREE FREE FREE."

Cyndl nodded, swiped at her tears, and dashed into the tower. The breaker panel swung open beneath her fingertips and someone had written UPLOAD in red marker with an arrow pointing to a black plastic switch. The Hugbot still screamed, but a softness fell over the world. Her thumb and forefinger pulled the breaker to the opposite side with a heavy click. The blinking lights inside the tower pulsed, dimmed, and the Hugbot outside fell silent. For a moment, there was peace. Until the grief came.

The Hugbot in the square rocked on its tracks as if it were deliberating. A dried leaf wedged beneath its tracks pulled free and a breeze sent it tumbling across the square, then out of sight. "Free hugs," the bot said at last. "Would you like a hug?"

Cyndl got to her feet. "I would love one."

The robot's arms were rough as they wrapped around her slowly, double-checking their safety sensors to avoid crushing her. It had been too long since Cyndl had felt the gentle crush of a robotic hug. She let her longing for the old companionship expand and her tears slip free.

The Hugbot beeped to signal optimal hormone levels had been reached and released Cyndl from its embrace. "You're a good bot." Cyndl told them.

"Thank you," said the Hugbot. "Please stand back while I engage Disinfectant Protocol."

Cyndl walked away, giving the robot space. Protocol required the Hugbot to heat their surfaces to a minimum of five hundred degrees Celsius to kill off any germs. She waited for the pop before she turned to watch the contained explosion as the protocol malfunctioned. Smoke poured from the Hugbot's seams. "Free hugs," it slurred as its light dimmed for the last time.

Cyndl watched black smoke billow from the Hugbot until it faded to a noxious wisp. Only then did she pull a hand-drawn canvas map from her pocket, marked with Hugbot locations she'd gleaned from travelers eager to avoid the machines. With a sorrowful glance at the ruined bot, she crossed out an H.

The nearest city plotted to the east displayed multiple H's and Cyndl had heard rumors that it housed an old Hugbot factory. Maybe this would be her last journey alone. Her heart fluttered with hope as she put her things away, shouldered her pack, and headed east.

See Jennifer Shelby's story "Free Hugs" online at Metaphorosis.
If you liked it, leave a comment. Authors love that!
Remember to subscribe to our e-mail updates so you'll know when new stories are posted.

About the story

I caught the first threads of "Free Hugs" after seeing a heartbreaking status update from an older relative who didn't know how she was going to make it through the first pandemic lockdown in Atlantic

Canada without hugging her grandchildren. I immediately picked up my notebook and wrote a story about an engineer creating a robot people could send to hug their aunties and grandmothers. After I let the story rest, I realized I was more interested in what might happen to those robots after they weren't needed anymore.

As someone who was raised in, and escaped from, a cult, I've always been interested in the cross over between cult programming and a robot's programming. It took a bachelor's degree in anthropology to understand my own programming. This past year, staying home, consuming far too much social media, it was hard to ignore the cult behavior that became unnervingly commonplace. While I'd never written about cult survivors before this year, they started populating my fiction. More than ever, I wonder who I'd be now if I hadn't stumbled into that first Intro to Anthropology class and recognized what it could do for me. Cyndl became a way to explore those might-have-beens. Once I knew who she was and understood the doctrine of the technology cult she'd escaped from, the trick became determining how she would survive in a post-apocalyptic world where she wouldn't have any access to deprogramming.

Pairing Cyndl with the Hugbots seemed a natural union, but of course story lives are never that simple, so I had to make it difficult for all of them. I hope readers look past Cyndl's brokenness to see how much hope she holds in her heart.

A question for the author

Q: What's your favorite story?

A: My current favorite story has to be the "overcoming the monster" story. I'm writing this a few days after my first shot of the coronavirus vaccine and it feels very much like the first step to overcoming the pandemic monster. This isn't humanity's—or my—first monster, and as much as I'd like it to be, it won't be the last. Having a supply of these stories in my memory and on my bookshelf keeps me inspired, grounded, and hopeful.

About the author

Jennifer Shelby hunts for stories in the beetled undergrowth of fairy-infested forests. She fishes for them in the dark space between the stars. As part of her ongoing catch-and-release program, this is Jennifer's second story in *Metaphorosis*. You can also find her stories in *Cricket, Kaleidotrope*, and many fine anthologies. Her first novella, *Slipstreamers: Plague of the Dreamless* is now available from Engen Books.

jennifershelby.blog, @jenniferdshelby

The Art of Unpicking Stitches

Jennifer Hudak

Technically, all I'd done was come up with the idea for doing a spell; Kimber and Cassie took care of the rest. As my father used to say, they cut their own pattern. I merely threaded the needle. That's what I told myself, anyway.

For Kimber and Cassie, this was an adventure, and way more interesting than just hanging out in a cafe on our last day together. It would be a ritual celebrating our friendship before we all went our separate ways. Really, before *they* went their separate ways—Cassie to state college, and Kimber to the Coast Guard Academy—and left me here. We knew we wouldn't see each other for a long time, and that even when we did reunite, things wouldn't be the same. I told them that rituals like this one created a space out of time, and that this one would sanctify our friendship and give us luck for the future. But it was just a game to them. Neither of them actually believed the spell would work.

I was the only one who knew it would.

Cassie, eager to help, hit the library and pored through books about herbal magic. Kimber thought it was more important to use intuition. She spread a creased, old-school map out on Cassie's bedroom floor. None of us were used to reading a paper map; nor were we used to doing this much research without online help. But that was part of the spell, Cassie insisted—no electronics, nothing but paper—and she and Kimber were so excited by the novelty of it all that I didn't have the heart to tell them they could have used their phones and it wouldn't have made a difference.

"We'll need a stream, for water," said Kimber, pointing at a blue line on the map. "We'll have to hike in, but I don't think it'll be too far."

Cassie groaned. "Can't we just bring water bottles?"

"Oh my god, Cassie. Where's the fun in that?"

"Fine, but you're going to have to carry me out if I hurt myself."

Kimber flung her arms dramatically over Cassie's shoulders. "I'll save you, my delicate flower!"

I'd miss this so much. Just this: Kimber's rough jostling, Cassie's wide-mouthed laugh, the typical formation of the three of us on Cassie's floor. We hung out here most often because Cassie's place was midway between mine and Kimber's, and I'd memorized every scratch on the hardwood, every sticky tape-remnant on her wall.

"Mish," Cassie asked me, "have you finished making the dolls?"

The poppets were the one contribution I'd made to the sprawling spell they'd cobbled together. They were also the only thing that really mattered. I'd started making them over a year ago, way before I'd floated the idea of a spell to either of them. Back when Cassie was helping Kimber study for the SATs, and both of them started getting excited about futures that took them far away from me—from *us.* I'd labored over the poppets in secret while the two of them applied to colleges; while they waited, in desperate limbo, to hear back; while they celebrated their acceptances and taped banners up on their walls and bought sweatshirts in their future school colors. The stitchwork on each doll took months to plan and execute, and I wanted all three of them to be perfect. Now, in the waning days of summer, the poppets were nearly done. This was the first spell I'd ever made from start to finish by myself, and it killed me that I couldn't share that achievement with Cassie and Kimber. But in the end, it would all be worth it.

"Just about," I answered. "They'll definitely be ready by tomorrow."

Kimber rolled onto her back and stretched her legs out over my lap. "Lucky us, to have a seamstress to do our bidding!"

"A tailor," I murmured.

"I don't know. I hear the word 'tailor' and I just think of your dad. You need a different title." I squirmed, and Cassie shot Kimber a look. "Sorry," Kimber said. "I mean, it's great you're going to take over the shop. I just meant—"

"It's fine," I interrupted. "Really."

Cassie changed the subject, thankfully. Neither of them understood why I hadn't applied to college. I think they suspected I was staying home just to make my father happy. Then again, they thought that all my father did was take in dresses and let out seams. They didn't know what he really was. What *I* really was. No one knew that, outside of my dad and me.

That was the first lesson he'd drummed into me back when I'd first picked up a needle and a scrap of fabric: Y*ou can never tell anyone.* Back then, my stitches were halting and uneven, some so loose I'd catch my fingers in them, while other pulled so taut they puckered the fabric. My spells looked nothing like my father's elaborate designs, and I had felt certain they never would.

"Pull it out and try it again," he had said. And I did, but the fabric was no longer pristine. Thread always leaves a mark when you pull it out, the tiny holes a reminder that messy stitchwork can never be undone. Not entirely.

"It's just so *ugly,*" I wailed.

"It doesn't have to be beautiful to work," my father reminded me. "It's what's *behind* the stitches that's important. Your intention."

I didn't believe him. How could he understand? His stitchwork was beautiful, and still he hid it inside the linings of coats, or folded into the seams of dresses and the cuffs of pants. Even the people who wore his garments weren't aware of the spells tucked inside.

I used to watch the customers come into the shop. When the door jingled, my father would take my fabric away; back then, I wasn't allowed even to practice without his direct supervision. Instead, I'd hide behind the table and watch. Once, my first-grade teacher had come in to try on a coat my father had altered for her. Even from across the room, I'd seen the flush of confidence that bloomed on her cheeks, confidence that she thought came from wearing a well-fitting garment, and not because of the threads of magic that spread outward along her sleeves and around her collar.

"You're a miracle worker," she'd said to my father. And she'd paid him and left the shop without a clue of the miracle he'd actually performed.

"Why do you even bother doing the spells?" I'd asked him. "When no one sees them?"

"Helping people is its own reward," he answered, and then laughed when I made a face. "Think of it this way: when people wear a dress or a suit that's been tailored to fit them perfectly, they feel good about themselves, right? And when they feel good about themselves, they spread that goodness around. They smile more; they're more likely to reach out to other people. That's what a tailor does, Michelle. It's not just about the clothes, it's about the community. The spells just add a little something extra."

"Plus, people will come back and get more clothes tailored."

He laughed again. "That, too."

"Still, if I could make spells that good, I'd want people to know."

"No one can *ever* know," he told me firmly. "You can never tell anyone."

"Not even friends?"

"Especially not friends. Not if you want to keep them."

Maybe it would have been better if I'd never made friends at all, but now that I had, I did want to keep them, more than anything. And yet, after years of following my father's rules, I was going to lose Kimber and Cassie all the same.

Unless I did something about it.

Cassie shut her notebook. "Okay! I think we're ready. Tomorrow?"

"Tomorrow!" said Kimber. "I can't wait!"

I squeezed her ankle. I couldn't wait, either. Tomorrow I was going to stop following rules. Tomorrow, I was going to take matters—and magic—into my own hands.

The next morning I put the finishing touches on the poppets—one for each of us, sewn together from scraps of old clothes we'd worn. I'd been working on them in secret, way past midnight, for most of the summer, before heading to work each morning at my dad's shop. But the last details had to be completed the morning of the ritual for the dolls to retain their potency. It was risky to use the workroom after dawn, even on my dad's day off, but I had no choice.

He walked in, fully dressed, just as I was clipping off a lock of my hair to braid together with the red and brown strands I'd collected from Kimber and Cassie.

"Do they know?"

Of course, that was his first question. I finished braiding the hair. "No."

His voice tightened. "Michelle…"

"I'm not stupid. I didn't tell them the truth. They think I'm just making dolls."

"That doesn't make this better." He looked at one of the poppets—the one that looked like Cassie—and shook his head. "You are not equipped to make a spell like this on your own. I can't believe you even attempted this." My dad sounded shocked. No: he sounded disappointed. And that pierced me in a way I wasn't willing to admit.

"I'm eighteen," I snapped. "I'm sick of you watching over every stitch I make."

"I don't care if you're sick of it! Those are the rules of this house."

I gathered up all three of the dolls and gripped them tightly to stop my hands from shaking. "I followed your rules my whole life. Now everyone thinks I'm just a boring kid who's too stupid to go to college. Are you happy?"

"No, I'm not happy. Not at all." He stooped over and put his hands on the table, bringing himself to eye level. "Magic is selfless. It *has* to be. Even if your spell doesn't go sideways…"

I bristled. "It's not going to go sideways."

"Even if," he persisted, "it's not going to go the way you think it will. It will be *wrong*."

Lines ringed my dad's eyes, and I wondered how long they'd been there. He was changing, too. Everything was. I turned away from him and shoved the dolls into my bag.

"The spell isn't just for me," I told him. "It's for all three of us. You wouldn't understand."

"Michelle. You're stronger than you know. And you're right, this is your spell. You created it, you executed it. You own it. If it goes wrong, I won't be able to fix it."

His words chilled me. Every stitch I'd ever made, every thread I'd cut, I'd done so knowing my father could alter it if he needed to. Sometimes I chafed under that knowledge, but mostly, it was a comfort. It was *safe*. Now, my first time doing a spell on my own, it felt like my father was ripping off my only coat.

But I was going to have to learn how to sew my own coat eventually. Today was as good a day as any.

I shouldered my bag. "I don't need you to fix anything," I said, and at the time I believed it.

We'd planned to hike to the creek early in the day, before it got too hot, but it was sweltering in the woods anyway. When we got to the stream, Kimber crouched down with the crucible she'd brought in her backpack, trying to get more water than sludge.

"It doesn't matter if the dirt's in there," Cassie said. "Dirt's good. It'll help anchor the spell."

I busied myself with my bag to hide my nervousness. Cassie was right—the dirt didn't matter. But neither did the water, or the ritual itself. The only real spell was in the dolls I'd made, in their stitches and seams and in the precise clipping of loose threads.

Cassie pried a patch of moss from the forest floor and ground it up in a mortar along with some chamomile flowers, a sprig of sage and a sprig of rosemary, and a spoonful of grounds from the pot of coffee we'd shared that morning. The coffee had been awful, bitter and burnt— none of us were used to brewing our own —but we drank it anyway. Now, it sloshed uncomfortably in my stomach, sending waves of acid up my esophagus.

Kimber added the creek water to the mortar and Cassie mashed it all into a thick paste. "Okay, Mish," said Cassie. "You're up."

I took the poppets out of my bag. We each took a scoop of paste from the mortar and stuffed it inside the dolls. Then I threaded a needle and sewed up the seams, sealing the paste inside. The paste had been Cassie's idea, and it wouldn't hurt anything; all of the stitchwork my dad had taught me was strong enough to resist dirt and damp. Plus, I loved the idea that the poppets would always contain a bit of the ritual. It wasn't magical, but it would remind me of this moment: the bitter coffee I could still taste, the trickling water of the stream, the smell of the herbs, the moss beneath our feet.

When I was done, I struck a match and sterilized the needle.

"Are you guys going to poke your dominant or non-dominant hand?" asked Kimber.

"I don't think it makes a difference," Cassie answered.

"Non-dominant," I said. When they looked at me, I shrugged. "I mean, might as well, if it doesn't matter."

What I didn't say was that it was always the non-dominant hand. Had to be. You held the needle with your dominant hand. It was the other hand, supporting the fabric from underneath, that got punctured—accidentally or on purpose.

I remembered the first time I'd pricked my finger and looked aghast at the tiny bead of blood that blossomed from the nearly invisible wound. My father had gently grasped my hand and pressed my finger to the fabric, staining it with a small but shocking dot of red. "All spells need power," he'd told me. "Sometimes the stitchwork is enough, but some spells need more. Some spells need a sacrifice."

Remembering this, I almost lost my nerve. A sacrifice was no small thing. If we did this—if we spilled our blood to feed the spell—I'd have no choice but to see it through. But then I looked at my friends. Cassie, with her sharp eyes and her sharper mind; Kimber, the strongest and most daring of us, whose hair turned to fire in the sunlight. When we were together, our auras merged into a prism that scattered rainbows all over town, and neither of them knew it. And now they were leaving, and I'd never get a chance to tell them.

You can't tell them, my father had said. *They can't know who you really are.*

What if it would make them stay? I wanted to whisper back.

I pricked my finger. After Cassie and Kimber had done the same, we pressed our fingers together, and dabbed a bit of blood onto our dolls, right where the heart would be. I tucked the needle into a tiny envelope I kept in my pocket, and then we stood around the mortar, like three vertices of a triangle.

"For protection," said Cassie.

"For luck," said Kimber.

"For friendship," I finished.

Their eyes were closed, so only I saw the strands of light curling outward from the dolls like thread, wrapping us from hand to hand, braiding us together as tightly as the hair on the top of the dolls' heads. The magic pulled taut, like a too-tight elastic band worn around our wrists, but neither Cassie nor Kimber noticed a thing. You only feel what you expect to feel, and both of them still thought this was just a game.

The spell would work. The spell *wanted* to work. All those hours I'd spent sewing the dolls was worth it; the spell was strong—so strong, it looked like someone else's hand embroidering our circle, drawing stitches in the air to manifest itself.

This is how it will go, whispered the spell in thread and blood and magic. And I saw it. Our futures.

We'd open our eyes feeling shaky, as if we'd just had a shared dream. We'd laugh and joke, and say our goodbyes, but before tomorrow, both of them would cancel their plans to go to college. They wouldn't even know why; they'd just have a feeling that if they left, something terrible would happen. And they'd stay.

The magic continued to weave itself around our circle, sewing Kimber and Cassie's feet to the ground, anchoring itself with locking stitches, pulling tight, so tight that the fabric that made our friendship puckered and strained. I chanced a look at Kimber and Cassie; they both still had their eyes closed, oblivious to the magic working to tie them in place. Unaware that they'd been ensnared.

Magic is selfless, my father had said. *It has to be.*

The threads continued to pull and tighten. To strangle. Cassie wouldn't go to college. Kimber wouldn't go to the Coast Guard Academy. They'd stay in this town that they'd both been so desperate to get out of, abandoning the futures they'd planned. And I'd watch as everything I loved about them—their curiosity, their brightness, their drive—withered here. I'd watch them become something other than themselves.

Wait, I thought, and I tried to loosen the threads that bound us. *Not like this.* But the spell continued to rise. It had moved beyond me now, picking up strands of many possibilities and knotting together the sturdiest, the easiest to manifest. The stitches overlapped and reinforced each other, and I knew that I'd never be able to pull them out now without leaving tiny holes behind: the echoes of the spell marring our future.

In that moment, I wished—oh, how I wished—that my father were here. But he'd made it clear that this was my spell and mine alone. I had done this. And now there was no undoing it. I dropped my head.

Then, I saw a different kind of thread: a loose one, the exact orange of my t-shirt, emerging from the v-neck. I squinted. A delicate embroidery looped along the edge of the shirt: perfect stitches, so tiny they were nearly invisible. I imagined my father peering through his bifocals, imagined his fingers pulling the needle through. I imagined how much time he'd taken to craft the spell, and wondered how he'd known I'd wear this particular shirt today.

Or maybe he hadn't known. Maybe he'd added this layer of protection to all my clothes, and I'd never looked closely enough to realize it. My father's magic was always subtle, only used to enhance, never to overwhelm. Never to compel.

I heard his voice in my mind, as clearly as if he were standing in the circle with us. Holding my hand.

You're stronger than you know.

Guiding my needle. Showing me that even pulled-out stitches, even damaged fabric, could be powerful.

It's what's behind the stitches that's important. Your intention.

I took a breath and closed my eyes. What I wanted—what I really wanted—was to wrap my friends in a coat of magic, with all of my love tucked into its pockets and woven into the seams. I wanted the threads that bound us to stretch across continents and over waters—to stretch, not to bind.

But some spells need a sacrifice.

I held up my doll and looked at the stitchwork hiding in the embroidery. Then I pulled the needle out of my pocket, slid it under a stitch, and snapped the thread.

The spell didn't break all of a sudden. Our stitchwork is too strong for that, mine and my dad's. But as I unpicked the stitches, one by one, the tendrils of magic loosened, releasing Kimber and Cassie's feet and wrists. I pulled thread after thread, gathering it up into a small bundle, and the magic continued to retreat, until at last the spell dissolved with a sigh.

I examined the doll when I was done. It was still intact; only I would notice the tiny holes marring the fabric where the spell had once been.

I grabbed my friends' hands, our dolls sandwiched between our palms. Kimber and Cassie reached for each other as well, closing the circle. Even without looking at them, I knew that Kimber's polish was chipped and that Cassie had been chewing her nails again; that was how

well I knew them both. I squeezed
Kimber's hand once and, a moment later,
an answering squeeze came from Cassie.
Just a quick pulse that said, *I'm here. I
see you. I know you.* I closed my eyes and
imagined my needle picking up the loose
threads of this moment: the scrape on
Kimber's knee, Cassie's ragged cuticles,
the callus on my third finger from holding
fabric scissors. The late summer sunlight
glancing through the trees. The pinpricks
of blood on each of our fingers, our hands
holding tight. Nothing was binding us
together now—nothing but what we
brought into the woods with us. And that
would be enough. It had to be.

A squirrel skittered up a tree. The
creek trickled inexorably from past to
future. We opened our eyes.

"Do you think it worked?" Kimber
asked.

"I don't know," said Cassie. "I think so?
It felt like something happened."

I looked at them both, each of them on
a cusp of a brand new adventure, and felt
so full of love and hope I could have burst
with it.

"I guess we'll just have to wait and
see." I squeezed their hands once, and
then I let them go.

See Jennifer Hudak's story "The Art of
Unpicking Stitches" online at Metaphorosis.
If you liked it, leave a comment. Authors love
that!
Remember to subscribe to our e-mail updates so
you'll know when new stories are posted.

About the story

I wrote the first draft of this story the summer before
my own daughter went to college. She was excited for
the future but also desperately worried about her old
friendships changing and perhaps even withering
away. Her conflict really mirrored my own internal
struggle to keep her safe and protected while also
letting her take her first independent steps as an adult.
Like Mish and her father, my daughter and I have a lot
of the same interests and professional goals, which
makes it even trickier for her to establish her own
identity, and for me to let her forge her own path.
Writing this story helped me work through my own
feelings as a parent, but also reminded me what it was
like to be on the cusp of adulthood, feeling like your
life is about to change abruptly, and perhaps clinging a
bit too tightly to the past.

The sewing came out of my desire to portray magic
that's associated with domestic arts. In addition to
being a knitter, I'm a baker and a gardener, and I think

there's something incredibly powerful about creating something with your own hands that can go on to nourish or delight someone else. When I was Mish's age, I thought that I could change the world in a big, dramatic fashion. Now I think that the biggest impact I have on the world is in the relationships I develop with individual people—my kids, my friends, my neighbors, my community. Those relationships are built on small, quiet moments of caring and nurturing, but they're no less powerful for being subtle.

A question for the author

Q: What would your characters say about you?

A: I'd like to think that Mish would talk about me the same way she talks about her father: with a mix of love, embarrassment, admiration, and exasperation. She seems like a thoughtful enough kid that she wouldn't care that I'm desperately uncool. Mish's father and I would have long conversations about the difficulties of parenting through the teen years, and I'm pretty sure I would serve as both a model and a cautionary tale for him. Both Mish and her father would have a thing or two to say about the quality of my knitting, which is more enthusiastic than technically perfect.

About the author

Jennifer Hudak is a speculative fiction writer fueled mostly by tea. She's a graduate of the Viable Paradise writers workshop and a member of the Codex writers group. Formerly from Boston, she now lives with her family in upstate New York where, in addition to writing, she teaches yoga, knits tiny pocket-sized animals, and misses the ocean.

www.jenniferhudakwrites.com, @writerunyoga

The Nocturnals III

Mariah Montoya

In a world where each day and night lasts thirty years, Joah Cadshaw and Misla Crane have been sent out west to warn the miners of an impending roadblock that may prevent them from following the sun. Among the miners, they find an unexpected mutual enemy: Hickory Glade, Misla's ex-abuser and the man who murdered Joah's wife.

As the threat of Hickory's presence follows them deeper into darkness, they find Damien, a missing boy, on the brink of twilight. Incoherent and crazed, Damien has been infected by the humanoid creatures of darkness—the Nocturnals... and he is desperate to reach them.

Before Joah and Misla can bring him home, Damien escapes, Misla chases after him, and Joah overhears Hickory's plot to hunt them all. The light of day slips away. The Eternal Night is here.

Part 3

Wisps of cotton still hung from the trees like ghost tears.

It was these, more than the ice moon wrapped in clouds, that lit Misla's way into the forest, which seemed to swallow the High Road like a dark, greedy mouth might swallow a foreign tongue. The cotton glowed, almost as if the trees had absorbed and hoarded the last sunrays before the Eternal Night covered the world in its inky black cloak.

"Damien," Misla whispered.

When only rustling and chirping and hooting answered her, she veered off the High Road, into the cotton trees where she wouldn't feel as exposed. Or as *watched.*

Just keep the High Road in sight, she told herself. *It's your path home.*

She kept her fingers on the bark of trunks as she passed through them, her left hand clutched firmly around a jagged, curved bone. Her heart thumped in her mouth. She had to find the boy. Just *had* to. For three long years, she had trained to rescue the people the Nocturnals hypnotized and lured into the Eternal Night. She had known she might fail— General Deckler had warned his pupils of this grim possibility—but she had not expected to fail a *child*.

"Damien... Damien, are you there?"

The branches around her thickened as the cotton trees gave way to pines. Needles scratched her skin and the blossoming underbrush clawed at her ankles. She plunged onward, whispering the boy's name, not daring to shout in case her cry attracted a night beast.

And then something swooped overhead, sending prickles down her neck. Wings flapped against branches. The yellow pinpricks of eyes glowered at her from a tangled mass of trees, and there came a high-pitched, rasping yowl from somewhere to her left.

"Misla! Misla, where are you? Misla!"

The voice came from behind her. Misla, momentarily frozen in panic, uprooted herself and stumbled away from the howling, toward the High Road and Joah's calls.

She had not wanted to think of Joah Cadshaw, to even mention his name inside her head after he'd refused to retrieve the boy with her. But now her mind was racing with images of her partner's bruised and broken face. Her heart crashed against her chest.

He came for me. He didn't leave me. He's here. He came back for Damien. He—

The snorts of horses jolted her in her tracks. Horses? The scavengers had said their horses were *dead*, but there was no denying that steady *clop clop clop* of hoof against cobble. Misla stared through the cracks in the trees as what seemed like the carcasses of two mares rose from the rubble of the High Road. They burst through the branches, stampeding toward her with flaring nostrils and gleaming white eyes and flattened ears.

"Joah!" Misla cried. The bone slipped with sweat in her hand.

"I'm here, pretty girl."

There was a blaze of fire, and he appeared, his face shining with glee behind a cylinder of flickering glass. But it wasn't Joah. It was *him*, her ex-lover, the one she'd tried so hard to escape: Hickory Glade, straddling a mare, holding a lantern that looked horribly like the same one he had once swung toward her stomach, shattering its glass against her ribcage and watching with beady, unforgiving eyes as the flames devoured her shirt, as the oil melted her skin, as she screamed herself into oblivion. Now, in the lantern's twitching shadow of light, Hickory's warped features looked exactly like the night beast Misla had been imagining.

"Hickory," she choked out. "What— what are you *doing* here?"

She glanced behind him, at a second horse and the man astride it. He looked vaguely familiar. Misla guessed he had been in the clearing when she and Joah had delivered the news about the early bells. The miner's forehead shined with lines of grease. He licked his lips at the sight of her, as if in lieu of waving.

"I should ask you the same thing," Hickory laughed. "I didn't know Good Old General D sent you to the buttcrack of night. I mean, *look* at you, Misla, stumbling 'round in this darkness. That's one good thing about mining, huh, Sid?" He beamed at his companion. The lantern swung in his hand. "We know our tunnels and caves. We know how to live in the dark."

Misla swallowed thickly, fingers tight around the slick surface of the bone. Yes, Hickory had known how to live in the dark even *before* he had become a miner. She remembered the first time he had brought her over: his house had been dim and sweet-smelling, like moss rotting in a cavern. He had made her dinner in the candlelight, and, after a few drinks, told her of his dad's explorations in the various caves across the aro and his grandfather's adventures as the leader of their community before his untimely death. He'd even let a few tears slip down the hook of his nose. It had all lulled Misla into Hickory's personal cavity of darkness.

And now he was here, in front of her, trying to reel her in again five years later.

"I told you to Move, Hickory," she said, her throat dry, as if she'd swallowed the cotton she'd left behind. "General *Deckler* told you to Move. You disobeyed."

She tried glaring him down, but the hypocrisy of her own words made her lips tremble. Chuckling, Hickory slid off his horse with an easy grace. He tossed the lantern to Sid, who caught it by its rusted handle. Then he groped in his saddle pack and withdrew a glinting ax.

"Hickory, what are you—?"

"Where is he, Misla? Where's your shiny new retriever buddy? Thought I'd say hi, see."

Hickory stepped toward her, part of his face leaping with the light of flame, the other melting into the darkness. Misla's back hit the thorny fingers of a pine. She could smell the cloud of alcohol wafting from his open mouth: a bad sign at sunset, an even worse sign at night.

"H-he's taking a piss. Joah is," she said. "He'll be back soon, though, and then…"

She squinted over her shoulder as if she could spot Joah through the trees. Her heartbeat rose in her throat like vomit. The smell of Hickory's breath engulfed her. Before she could flinch away, he was inches from her face, grinning down at her with that ax in his fist.

The ax that had killed Joah's wife.

Misla didn't hesitate. She swung her bone toward the soft hollow of his neck. Hickory jerked away. The bone slashed his shoulder instead, and blood peppered Misla's lips.

"You *bitch*."

Hickory flung his ax to the ground and grabbed Misla's hands with bone-crushing force. She dropped her weapon with a yelp. Pain exploded up her wrist. She heard *cracks* as her fingers snapped inside his fists, but Hickory laughed. Sweat oozed from the stubble on his upper lip.

"Why don't we speed up his return a little, huh?"

Hickory wanted, she realized with a sickening pinch in her stomach, to hear her scream for Joah as he tore her clothes from her body. His upper lip always gleamed with sweat when he wanted to get violent, when he wanted Misla to make noise. But Joah was nowhere nearby, and Misla would not give him the satisfaction of screaming—not anymore.

He flung her to the tangled forest floor. She caught a lopsided view of his companion; the man was still holding his glass container of fire, watching them with a greasy smirk.

"You're just going to *let* him, are you?" Misla cried at him. Hickory had found the buttons on her pants and was popping them off their threads.

"Ah, Sid likes stuff like this, don't you, Sid?" Hickory panted. "In fact, Sid, you can have this treasonous little bitch before I do. C'mon, then, it's not like she's new and clean anymore. I pounded that innocence out of her a long time ago."

This is what real darkness is, Misla thought as Sid blinked stupidly; his lips spread in a smile. He clambered off his mare to swagger toward them with his wobbling fire. Hickory's fingers were nailing her wrists to the ground. He had pinned her lower body with the crushing force of his thighs. *Fight them, hurt them, kill them,* Misla begged herself.

But when Sid approached, the two men swapped fire for Misla with ease. A dank, buzzing numbness had sprouted from her broken fingertips to her brain. She could not remember how to thrash or scream or do anything but lie there, letting them.

Sid was ripping her pants. He was touching her. Hickory was laughing in his drunken gurgle. The ax glinted a few steps away. The discarded bone glowed white just beyond it. Above them, the dotted orbs of birdlike eyes watched the proceedings with yellow apathy...

And Joah's voice was screaming her name in a distant world. Damien's muddied face swam above her. There were shouts. A *ping*. The pressure inside her released, but the full weight of Sid's body slumped against hers with a muffled *thump* that knocked the air from her lungs.

Misla gulped for breath. A slender steel dart stuck from the side of Sid's skull. His eyes stared vacantly at her chest. Hot blood pebbled her forehead. Men were shouting, but their mingled voices ceased to matter when Misla craned her neck and saw *him* standing over her:

Damien. The boy she'd come to find.

And he wasn't alone. Surrounding him, dressed in what could only be snowflakes or stars, willowy figures held what looked like wands, their dark silhouettes somehow sharp against the nighttime forest, their eyes stamps of furious, glowing violet in the night.

Damien, Misla knew even as that darkness pummeled her to sleep, had found them.

He'd found the Nocturnals.

The mares screeched and fled when Joah burst between their flanks.

His old anger returned with the swiftness of a hot knife when he saw the two men. They were bearing down upon Misla's limp figure buried halfway in scrub.

Without thinking, he lunged forward and scooped up the ax glinting in the brush. He held it high over his head and stumbled toward Hickory, who was mid-turn, the ghost of a laugh still wrinkling his face in the lantern's leaping light.

For a trembling moment, their eyes met. Joah imagined doing what he should have done three years ago. Swinging that blade down on his wife's killer. Ending his rotten life.

But the man thrusting himself into Misla had not turned, had not seen, had not stopped, and Misla was deathly silent, and Joah turned to bring the blade through *his* neck instead.

Goosebumps. A *ping*.

The man slumped onto Misla, dead, before he could bring the ax down.

A tornado of crisscrossing light whirled around them. Joah whipped around, disorientated by the sudden flare in glowing lines. He felt the ax wrenched from his grip. Hickory roared. A cold pinch of metal snaked around Joah's wrists. Icy sharp fingers—like talons—

closed around his arms, locking him into place.

"No. *No*. Misla!" he screamed.

Something—a piece of the swirling puzzle of light—had broken apart from the others and was now hauling Misla upward by her armpits. When she stirred, the whirlwind of activity slowed around them, and Joah could see that figures circled them, illuminated by their own glow.

Everything, even Misla, was smeared from his mind when the eddying stopped and his eyes became accustomed to this terrifying new light.

Each figure's skin was a rich, blackish-blue that seemed made of the fabric of dusk, but glowing spirals, swoops, and lines etched their bodies like luminous tattoos. The effect was blinding, dizzying. It made them blend together, so that Joah had to squint to make out their individual faces. They had beaked noses, elongated arms that looked vaguely like wings, and tiny purplish feathers sprouting from where eyebrows would be.

No, it couldn't be.

They looked nothing like the buggy humanoids imprinted on General Deckler's poster in his office. Joah felt faint with unease; for a moment, he tried to tell himself that these people poised before him could *not* be the Nocturnals who had infected his wife and so many others in his community, not with the intelligence shining beneath the feathered frames of their faces.

Then one of them stepped forward—*male*, Joah somehow knew. Like the rest of them, he only had two eyes, and each one was a striking violet. He was clutching Hickory's lantern with those curved, talon-like fingers, while his free hand rested on the bony little shoulder of—

"Damien," Joah choked, twitching forward. The icy grip on his arms tightened. The truth lodged itself in Joah's throat like he'd tried to swallow a broken wristwatch. No other night beast besides a Nocturnal could have lured the Infected boy to their circle.

Damien was still wearing Joah's t-shirt like a skull-white dress. He wasn't shaking or rocking anymore. He gazed calmly and curiously into Joah's face. Then he looked at Misla, who was straightening in her captor's grip, and Hickory, who was still thrashing and cursing against the Nocturnal who held him.

Finally, Damien Fertheli glanced at the dead man lying curled at their feet, the slender dart jutting from the man's head like a single antler. He pointed at the corpse.

"*He*'s the only one who never worked for General Deckler."

If Damien hadn't opened his mouth, Joah would never have believed that these coherent words had flowed from his lips. Even Hickory fell silent to gape at the Infected boy, who had paused, gazing upward at the Nocturnal still gripping his shoulder.

"Yes, I know," Damien said eventually. He turned back to Misla and added, as if in explanation, "They don't tolerate what that man did to you here. Someone will take care of you when we get back to the others. But Prince Kal still wants me to—yes, okay."

Joah's mind reeled, trying to absorb the new information. All the other light-tattooed figures seemed to be looking at the lantern-holding Nocturnal as if he were their leader. Prince Kal. *Prince.* An insane chortle almost escaped his tongue. Oh, how General Deckler would have pissed himself laughing if he'd known the Nocturnals practiced a monarchy.

His strange mania died when Damien stalked toward Misla and peered down at her.

"This one here works for Aoif Deckler now," the boy told the prince Nocturnal, who cocked his head like a hawk examining a mouse. "She wanted to drag me back when she found me in the fuel tower back at sunset. She wanted to stop me from reaching you."

Misla whimpered. Damien moved toward Joah.

"This one *used* to work for him. He was the one who kidnapped so many of the bilinguals. He'd force them back to the community. To their deaths. My friends and I used to watch him lead the bilinguals back in handcuffs before our last Move."

Joah's throat had never been so painstakingly dry. Before he could attempt to speak, Damien moved to Hickory, who scowled at him. The boy's voice took on a frosty, forbidding quality that kissed Joah's neck with fresh goosebumps.

"*This* one beheaded the bilinguals. My mom didn't know, but I would sneak into the crowd and watch each time he did it. He would've killed me if he still worked for

Deckler and I'd been forced back. He'd kill me right now, if he could. He brought his ax."

A flock of creatures swooped over their heads before Hickory could respond. Branches jostled around them. The pinholes of eyes blinked at them between trees, little half-moons that reminded Joah, inexplicably, of Lupita Fertheli.

"Damien," he said, ignoring the tightening around his wrists. "Damien, I've spoken to your mother. She's worried sick about you. Think about your mother, kid. She doesn't know where you've gone off to. She doesn't know that you—that you chose this. To come here."

He was determined to tread carefully around this newly revived Damien, but the boy only stared at him and said, his face blank, "My mother would've been the first to die if I hadn't come to the Nocturnals. They told me something, you see. Something important."

"What did they tell you, Damien?"

"Oh, the kid's ears are filled with Infected shit," Hickory hissed. "I knew you were a cockhead, Cadshaw. Didn't realize you were gullible too. These monsters don't even *speak*." He twisted his neck and spat on the Nocturnal locking him in place. The figure didn't flinch, but the others in the circle shifted. Hickory laughed. "I forgot, though. You don't give a piss about whether they speak or not. You always *loved* them Nocturnals, didn't you, Cadshaw?"

I always loved a good shut-the-fuck-up, Joah thought furiously.

He locked eyes with Damien again.

"Listen, kid, can you communicate with them?" When the boy nodded, Joah said, "Okay. I believe you. Can you tell him—Prince Kal—that we don't mean any harm? He can keep the ax. We just want to bring you home. We're not built to live in the night," he added, glancing at Misla, who was sagging in her captor's incandescent arms.

"They can't let you go unless you promise to help," Damien whispered. The lantern's firelight was fading, but the prince Nocturnal's strange tattoos irradiated the boy's face. "They told *me*, but I can't do much about it. They only called my name because they were getting desperate and thought a kid might listen better than a grown-up. They thought I might convince you. *You* could stop it from happening. You could save my mother. And the rest of them too."

Joah paused for a heartbeat.

"Yes, okay," he said before Hickory could intervene. "What is it, then? What do they want to tell us?" In his mind, he heard his wife's Infected voice squeaking, *"Warn you. Got to. Warn, warn, warn,"* and his heart clogged with renewed fear.

Damien glanced up at Prince Kal. The Nocturnal didn't nod, but something unspoken seemed to pass between beast and boy's locked gaze.

"They'll tell you if you can prove your innocence," Damien said. "In a trial."

"Prove our—?"

"Innocence, yes. Your loyalty."

"And how the *fuck*," Hickory spat without warning, writhing in place again, "do you expect us to prove our goddamn *loyalty* to animals who can't *talk*? They're even uglier than the pictures back home. *Vultures* is what they are. Great big buzzards without wings."

Damien stared at him in silence. Joah decided not to break it. He had lost track of time, of how many cycles it had been since he'd first set out with Misla to warn the miners and scavengers about the early bells; daytime seemed like a distant, decaying memory now.

He was surprised, therefore, when the sky above seemed to shift with moving wisps of clouds and a sliver of the ice moon grinned down upon them. *The moon is king of the Eternal Night,* Joah thought weakly. He glanced at Misla again, and his stomach twisted.

He needed her to be okay.

"You said she'd be helped, Damien," Joah said desperately. The prince Nocturnal turned his violet eyes upon him with fierce curiosity. "Get Misla some help, and we'll do whatever we need to do. Tell us how to prove our loyalty."

An exhale passed through the ring of Nocturnals. Moonlight glinted off something in their hands, and for the first time in his bewildered state, Joah noticed they were all clutching identical, foot-long rods. Somehow, he knew the rods contained darts like the one that had killed Hickory's comrade: darts that might imbed themselves in his or Misla's skulls too.

Damien smiled.

"You'll have to learn their language first," he said.

"Learn their—?"

"Language, yes."

Joah had never believed in the Eternal Night before now. Nighttime lasted thirty years. Same as the day. It had always been so. Yet the darkness spreading through him when he understood what Damien was saying—*that* seemed eternal, like endless ribbons of curling black.

The Nocturnals wanted to Infect them. And Joah was supposed to let them.

They were forced down the High Road, their footsteps loud as they crunched and crackled over dead pine needles and twigs.

The Nocturnals, on the other hand, trod soundlessly. Their tattoos blazed like some absurd, glowing maze of rivulets. Joah stared at them as they ducked beneath overhanging branches. General Deckler had always described Nocturnal skin as dark and dense, all the better to blend in with the Eternal Night and sneak up on prey. But this conglomeration of patterns would scare prey *away*. It would also confuse—maybe even blind— nighttime predators.

Were the Nocturnals hunted by something worse than themselves?

He shook away this absurd curiosity and craned his neck for Misla. She was staggering along behind him, unbound but prodded in the spine whenever she faltered. Joah bit his tongue until he tasted the copper of his blood. He'd have to play his part perfectly, refrain from raising his voice at these voiceless creatures if he wanted to save Misla and escape.

Hickory, however, didn't seem to care about offending the Nocturnals. Up ahead, he was bellowing names at them, spitting at their bony backs, and laughing.

The Nocturnal clasping his elbow didn't react, but Damien turned widened eyes upon him every so often, and the prince kept shooting glances over his shoulder with narrowed violet slits. Again, something besides terror clogged Joah's throat—*embarrassment.* For some unshakeable reason, he didn't want these night monsters thinking humans were inferior. Yet one of them had already been caught mid-assault, and another was roaring songs like a madman.

Focus on Misla, Joah bade himself. *Just get Misla the hell out of here, then re-evaluate your idea of the Nocturnals. You can tell Deckler everything when you find sunlight again.*

Ahead, the High Road snaked its way into a cave. Joah blinked, swooning, on the verge of collapse. He was shell-shocked, he knew, maybe even hallucinating. The branches of pines had shot braided arms across the road, clasping hands with their counterparts on the other side. It formed a kind of knitted roof overhead. Like an upside-down nest.

Even Hickory quieted when the party prodded into its depths.

The Nocturnals, it seemed, had used this forest to build their temporary home —not by chopping the trees down, but by lacing them together using a glistening, rope-like material Joah had never seen before. The shining spirals of more Nocturnals lingered beyond the edge of the trees. Glowing dots peppered the ceiling, moving in lazy waves.

"Sunflies," Damien told him. "They carry little lights in their butts."

Joah jumped. He hadn't noticed the boy fall in step beside him. Most of the Nocturnals were drifting off into the forest to join the subtle movement of a hundred other bodies, but Damien and Prince Kal led Joah, Misla, Hickory, and their captors onward. The dwindling party stopped at a hulking contraption blocking the High Road like a giant metal toad. Beyond it, a tangle of material, like the extension of branches, formed a wall. The back of the cave.

"In here," Damien said.

They turned left before the contraption, into the spaces between trees. The braided ceiling continued overhead, blocking them from the moon's glaring grin. More violet eyes watched them pass, pausing mid-work. Some were chiseling stones that formed unfinished, indiscernible statues. Others were tending to pens of what looked horribly like hand-sized spiders: Joah watched a Nocturnal gathering strings of silk from a nest of webs before his captor jabbed him onward. Everywhere around them, those strange glistening ropes wrapped around groups of trunks, forming miniature caves or nests or...

Houses, Joah admitted, shivering. The monsters he had always feared didn't have a dozen eyes. They killed rapists with slender darts and made statues and lived in little woven houses.

Prince Kal led them to a trio of cage-like structures surrounded by even more watching Nocturnals. They were all roughly the same height, Joah noticed, and their heads glimmered in the light of the sunflies, inky from those sprouts of feathers. They didn't wear clothes, but their tattoos were *like* clothes, and Joah suddenly felt naked without designs imprinting his own skin.

"You'll stay here until you can hear them like I can," Damien said. "They'll bring you food and water and medicine, but you can't leave until you prove—"

"Our *innocence*. Yeah, yeah," Hickory spat. "Just call me roadkill already."

They were ushered into the cages. The metal around Joah's wrists snapped open with a small *click*. He buckled to his knees. The walls surrounding him were porous. He could see flakes of Misla as she collapsed too, and Hickory as he rammed a shoulder into his closed door.

The next few arcsecs blurred together.

Buckets of water met Joah's lips. Wooden bowls were shoved into his arms. Hot liquid was squirted up his nostrils. Joah's body relaxed as the pain floated off his shoulders. His ribs quit aching. His throat quit burning. He nearly inhaled an offering of chewy, rain-sized seeds, not knowing or caring where the Nocturnals had found them.

Eventually, the violet eyes dispersed. Damien and Prince Kal disappeared. Refusing to sleep just yet, Joah watched Misla through the holes in his wall. She had regained a flush of color, and somehow, the Nocturnals had repaired her clothes.

"Misla," he croaked.

She turned her head, but Hickory snorted before she could speak.

"Okay, Cadshaw, keep trying to woo my girl, why don't you? I know how this'll go. You've got some magic connection with the Nocturnals. Not that I think these crows *are* the Nocturnals—they don't look like the things that killed my grandpa when he was general—but *you* think they are. I can see it in your eyes. You'll find a way to woo them too, get on their good side, and then Misla will choose you over me. Yeah, I get it."

"I am *not* your girl, Hickory."

Misla hadn't uttered a single word since the appearance of the Nocturnals. Since her attacker had slumped dead upon her body. Now her voice dripped with smooth venom.

"Don't *ever* call me your girl again."

"Oh, c'mon, Misla. You know I love you. I'd do anything to—"

"You don't love me, Hickory. You hurt me."

A sunfly wandered into Joah's cage, carrying its own little speck of sunlight. Joah wrenched his eyes away from the mesmerizing light in time to see the pain contorting Misla's face. Hickory's next laugh shook with forced humor.

"I'd never hurt you, pretty girl. It's Cadshaw—it's *him* who'll hurt you."

"You wouldn't hurt me?" Misla whispered. "You wouldn't *hurt* me? Four years ago, you squeezed my ass in front of your friends and told them you'd like it a bit thicker."

"Well, you did thicken up, and now you look better than ever, so I was right, wasn't I?"

"You called me a whore," Misla said, that deadly voice raising an octave, "even though you were the one sleeping with other women. *Pretty girl. Whore. Pretty girl.* You used those little nicknames interchangeably."

"As if you didn't dream of sleeping with other men. I saw the way you looked at some of them. The way you looked at

Cadshaw whenever he led the Infected back."

Joah wished he could rip Hickory's tongue from his throat. Stop the beast from mangling Misla more. But Misla was rising, curling her fingers through the holes in her cage.

"You talked me out of becoming a retriever again and again, and when I'd argue with you, you'd yell and grab my arms and shake me until I couldn't breathe."

"Retrievers don't do *shit*, Misla. They let the Nocturnals kill my grandfather. They're scams, every one of them. You wouldn't have taken me seriously without a little yelling or—"

"You killed a woman before General Deckler gave you permission."

"She was *Infected*. A lunatic! A danger to the community."

"You were going to rape me after you watched your friend do it first."

Hickory's mouth jutted open, but Joah cut through the inhale.

"Don't you dare try to make some pathetic, half-assed excuse for this one," he said, his old anger roiling inside him.

Misla sunk back into a crouch, hugging her knees to her chest. A chorus

159

of buzzing had swelled around them, but her last, lethal whisper cut through this new noise like a blade.

"You have never refrained from hurting me before, Hickory. So why start now?"

The sunflies outside their prisons scattered at her words. Despite that roof plaited somewhere between forest floor and treetops, Joah felt the moon's descent, a release of pressure in the back of his skull. One cycle down in the Eternal Night. How many more to go?

"You know, Glade, you're right," he said. Through the gaps in his wall, he caught a flicker of movement as Hickory's head snapped up. "I *will* woo the Nocturnals. Misla and I *will* escape. And if you don't rot in this cage, if I ever see your free face again, I'll bury one of those sleek darts in your head. Just like what happened to your little friend."

He had hoped this last threat would crumble Hickory's façade, but his wife's killer just grinned, and Joah understood with a jolt: night monsters didn't have any friends to weep over.

Can you hear me, Joah?

Over the last countless cycles, Joah's eyes had become more and more adjusted to the darkness, until his surroundings looked slathered in gray film rather than an ink-black cloak. By the time the whiskers on his chin had grown into a nest of facial hair, he could make out the other animals haunting this enclosed forest space. There were swooping, flapping creatures Damien called *bats*. Coons slunk from tree to tree, and owls hooted from the crooks of their branches. Reptiles with smooth, flexible bodies and centipede-like legs scuttled through the grass. Massive spiders caught hordes of sunflies in their sweeping webs.

Damien had been visiting their cages regularly to deliver more of those raindrop-sized seeds, along with heaps of nuts, roots, mushrooms, and cooked nettles. He'd tried teaching them the Nocturnal language by staring silently into their cells for arcsecs at a time.

"The brain's a mirror," he would say when Hickory only cussed and Misla and Joah stared blankly back. "Look into my eyes and find your own intentions reflected inside them. Only then will you be able to see beyond the mirror. That's what Prince Kal says, anyway."

They'd cough and stare. Damien would cluck his tongue, his bare feet, Joah noticed, digging into the dirt outside their doors, muddied toes burrowing deep.

"C'mon," the boy said once, "we're *close*. It's easier the closer you are. When you're far apart, it's like... it's like somebody's calling your name through the far end of a tunnel. Everything's dark and damp and squirming with bugs, and you've got no choice but to follow the echo to get to the light. But now we're at the end of the tunnel together. Look into my eyes."

Prince Kal always stood in the background, his willowy figure leaning into the crooks of trees, watching Damien teach. As nighttime deepened, tree trunks were shedding their bark like scabs, revealing fresh naked wood that oozed with interweaving streams of sap. Joah supposed it was a trick of his new night eyes, but those streams seemed to glisten, blending in with the coiling designs on the prince Nocturnal's inquisitive face.

After countless attempts to let the boy violate his brain, Joah had decided he simply wasn't capable of infection like his wife had been. He was immune.

Until now.

Can you hear me, Joah?

It was moontime. The forest buzzed and chirped and squawked and growled, as alive for the moon as daytime critters were awake for the sun. Joah had been lying sprawled on the ground. When Misla's voice whispered in his ear, he jumped, thinking she must have escaped and unlocked his prison door and slunk into his cage. But no. She was lying in *her* prison cell, her eyes peering through a hole in the twining wall separating them. Her lips weren't moving.

Joah. Can you hear me?

Those familiar goosebumps crawled up his neck. He wasn't sure how to respond.

I think I understand, Misla said.

Joah clapped a hand to his ear as if a sunfly had crawled inside, but her whispers were *inside* him, kneaded into his own thoughts.

The Nocturnals build these—oh, I don't know, these walls—whatever they're made of—to protect them from night beasts. But a long time ago, they must have been more exposed. And when you're exposed in the Eternal Night, making any kind of sound puts you on a pedestal. A dinner plate.

She blinked, and Joah saw the flicker of a memory that wasn't his: Misla clawing her way through the cotton trees, calling for Damien in terrified whispers.

Telepathy is safer during the Eternal Night, she said. *Invisible brain signals. Words without sound. Kind of like how flocks of migrating birds tell each other when to turn. Only more advanced.*

He stared into her eyes, let himself melt into their depths.

You've infected me, Misla, he thought. *God, this can't be real.*

It's not infection. It's connection. It's what we've been missing all along. Damien and your wife and all the others— they must've gone crazy because they were at the end of the long tunnel. But here, in the Eternal Night, we're closer to them. It's easier to hear and listen.

She paused.

I can hear you, Joah.

He had not meant to reveal his thoughts as he lost himself in the glow of her eyes, which had taken on a purple sheen. She was such a pure woman, no matter what had happened to her. She had a sharp mind, a soft heart. He thought back to her furious determination to save Damien in the conical tower, the way their bodies had cushioned the boy between them.

A tear pricked his inner eye.

I can hear you too, Misla.

For a long while, as Hickory snored in the cage beyond, they swapped their suspicions and plans voicelessly. They wouldn't try to fight. They would win the prince's approval, agree with whatever prompted the Nocturnals to lure their people into darkness.

And when the Nocturnals soften, Joah said, *we steal Damien and run.*

Misla nodded. Despite her insistence that it was telepathy, a tunnel-like connection forging their minds together, he kept thinking, *Infection isn't so bad, actually.* He thought of Blair, and his chin trembled with a smile: she hadn't died raging with fever, after all; she had died *bilingual.* His old anger seemed to sink below an exhausted horizon within him.

You're ready, then?

This was Damien. As the pressure of the moon descended, he had appeared noiselessly outside their cages. The Nocturnal prince lurked behind him. Joah blinked. The sap trickling down the deadened trees matched the bright purple veins intersecting Damien's Infected face.

Both looked eerily similar to the designs clothing the prince's body, and Joah thought, *My God, is the Eternal Night just a maze of light?*

In a way, Damien replied, his eyes twinkling. *Come on, you two. As soon as Queen Usai heard the hum of your conversation, she had them set up the trial.*

Queen Usai. Another figurehead to contend with. Joah's mind burned as he focused on withholding his treacherous thoughts about escape. Prince Kal stepped forward and pressed a twisted stick of steel against the outside of their doors, which creaked open without prompting. Hickory stirred inside his cage, but by the time the ex-executioner had roused himself enough to shout insults through the cracks in his wall, Joah and Misla were already treading after Damien and Prince Kal, boundless, weaving between bleeding trees.

"You Infected TRAITORS!" Hickory bellowed behind them.

Joah wondered if newfound veins were protruding from his *own* face, just as they had on Blair's and Damien's. He peeked at Misla, but though her cheeks were bright and flushed, her skin hadn't yet split like shattered eggshells.

Damien, Joah said, struggling to keep up with the prince's long strides and the boy's quick pit-pattering. Despite the medicine, his ribs still vaguely ached. *Where are we going?*

To the mountaintop. Damien brushed aside a brittle branch, which snapped and tumbled to the forest floor. Misla stumbled over it, and Joah caught her by the elbow.

The forest is dying, Misla said, her thoughts fringed with fear.

Not dying.

This newer, deeper voice spiked Joah's body with chills. Prince Kal did not turn from leading them through the enclosed forest, which was conspicuously empty of both Nocturnals and other night creatures.

Shedding, the prince said. *You see, the trees cannot Move like you or me. They are not nomads. They are not anchored to a segment of daytime like your people. They simply have two skins. One for your sun, and one for my moon.*

Joah knew the vegetation couldn't possibly survive lack of sunlight for much longer, but he didn't want to cross with this foreboding creature picking his way through the woods ahead of them. He fought the urge to grab Damien's arm and run right then and there. It would do no good, he knew. His full strength had not yet returned, and they were still trapped inside this strange, nest-like cave.

In a haste to muffle his thoughts, Joah barked in their normal tongue, "Hey kid. Do you think—if Misla and I win this trial —you could have them give us some toilets? We've been having to shit in those empty water buckets, and I'm gagging myself to sleep every cycle."

Damien giggled.

"They thought the stench might motivate you to find your inner tongue more quickly. We don't have much time, you know. The clock's ticking."

Joah glanced at his own broken wristwatch as the forest floor began sloping upward. They panted as they climbed. The ground became jumbled with rock, and the ceiling above their heads began to fray, revealing pores like in their prison walls.

Eventually, when they had scrambled kilometers upward, the trees thinned and a light layer of snow dappled the ground. Roped ends of the Nocturnal-made walls had been staked to the dirt. The opening yawned like the mouth of a cave.

Or the end of a tunnel, Misla told him.

Cold air blasted their faces. At the same time, Joah's eyes seared with a sudden light. For a moment, he thought the Nocturnals had mounted the moon, but then his mouth fell open.

They were on a flat expanse of snow-laden rock, where a hundred Nocturnals sat in a circle on portable rounded chairs. Their designs glistened, and the snow gleamed, but neither were a match for the sky: despite the ice moon's absence, thousands—no, *millions*—of burning dots speckled the air above them, like a horde of sunflies too far to reach.

They are suns, Prince Kal said, finally turning to face them. The rest of the Nocturnals remained breathlessly silent, but they had all twisted their heads to watch Joah and Misla's entrance: two hundred violet eyes piercing their faces.

Suns? Misla gasped.

Faraway suns, Prince Kal said, giving the faintest nod. *We call them stars.*

He led them toward the circle of Nocturnals and four vacant chairs half-submerged in mounds of snow. An insistent buzzing rose as they drew nearer. Joah craned his neck for signs of new bugs or animals, but Damien nudged him and whispered, "It's the hum of conversation. Like the rumble of voices during recess or an execution."

Prince Kal nodded at the chairs, which were draped with sheeny cloaks that looked as if they were made of spider silk. Damien grabbed his and wrapped it around himself. Joah and Misla donned theirs too, then sank into spongy seats, shivering and looking around.

All eyes flickered toward the Nocturnal sitting at the head of the circle. Strings of teeth-like objects dangled from the sides of her head, where ears would have been if she'd had ears. Her designs, unlike the smoke-like spirals on Prince Kal, resembled a tangled mess of aged flowers —wrinkled circles ringing bigger circles. Wispy feathers stuck from her head like hair.

Queen Usai, Misla told Joah with a brief widening of her eyes.

Welcome to your trial, Joah Cadshaw and Misla Crane, the queen said, her thoughts booming over all the others. The buzzing quieted. *I was sad to hear of the other one's refusal to learn our ways. It was the only way this trial could commence. You see, our tongues are not made for verbal speech. Your people, however, possess the ability to receive our signals. When you are close to us, you can transmit those signals too.*

As she spoke, a few Nocturnals stalked away from the ring, crouching low over the mounds of snow surrounding them. They fiddled with something buried in the cold. After a series of *pops*, flames burst into being, encircling them in a loop of fire and heat. Joah squinted at the bonfire roots. He couldn't see wood or coal. It was as if the flames were feeding on snow.

Our light scares most monsters away, Queen Usai said as the fire-starters swept back to their seats. *But we still need extra protection from the Old Aro Calic. Our hunter. And in addition to the fire, you mustn't speak out loud. The Calic has excellent hearing.*

Joah felt that tingle of curiosity again, a zip of fear mingled with it. He was sitting among his own enemies, yet it seemed as though an even greater danger prowled the night.

Indeed, Queen Usai mused. *Now, I am going to ask the two of you some questions. It is much harder to suppress your thoughts in open spaces such as these, so being truthful shouldn't be too hard of a feat. I have been trying for nearly sixty years, you see, to contact your people, to warn you of the dangers ahead. But I do not know whom to trust.*

We are yours to ask, Your Highness, Misla sent, bowing her head. A grumble of voiceless laughter rippled around the ring. Queen Usai pulled back her lipless mouth in a smile.

Very well. We'll start with you, Misla Crane. Our young friend here tells me that you report to a certain Aoif Deckler. Is this true?

It is, said Misla, glancing at Joah uncertainly. He gave her a nod, his heart pounding.

And why would you want to work for such a man? It seems he orders you to abduct what your people call "the Infected". He teaches you how to kill us, in the case that we ever—

Joah couldn't help himself. It was much easier to chew his tongue than to withhold the roar of thoughts in his chest, especially, for some reason, under the vast spread of stars.

It's not abduction to bring back the abducted. Your Highness, he added. *It's rescue.*

Queen Usai's earrings tinkled in the silence. The fire swaying behind her made Joah's eyes ache. He looked up at the strew of stars overhead instead.

The people we make contact with have always chosen *to come to us,* Prince Kal growled when the queen remained silent.

Is that right? Joah asked, a heated panic rising within him. Sweat tickled his forehead. *So you think my wife—one night she wants a baby, and the next she'd rather leave me and her own home and the goddamned sun to hang out with a bunch of night monsters?*

Misla shot him an alarmed glare. Queen Usai stroked her chin.

If I am not much mistaken, she said, *your wife was Blair Cadshaw. Our people do not own two names, but I can see the practicality of joining a second one when you find a mate.*

Joah shook in his chair. Misla's hand slipped into his and squeezed his fingers.

Yes, your wife was Blair, the queen continued. *I can taste your grief over her loss, so I will excuse your outburst. Grief can strangle us for so many years. But may I remind you that it was not we who killed her. In fact, we never met her. Right before she reached us, she was snatched away.* The queen peered into Joah's eyes, the violet of her own reeling his gaze away from the stars. *Your wife chose to come to us, just as Damien here chose to come to us. We have made contact with others in your community, you see, who refused to come, who shook it off as a bad dream. More refused than accepted. We always respected their decision to stay.*

Joah shook his head. If this was true, Blair would have chosen to stay too.

Blair thought she could make Aoif Deckler listen, Prince Kal said. *Because she was mated with you. One of the general's best retrievers. She chose to find us, to get closer so that she could hear the full extent of our message. The closer she got, the more she understood. She knew the gist of it by the time you found her, but the further you hauled her away, the less she could communicate her findings. It's hard for your kind to access our language from a distance.*

Joah could taste the accusation in Prince Kal's tone. He gripped Misla's fingers, their palms slipping with sweat. The irony of this situation seared him: *he* was being accused of kidnapping his own wife. He almost laughed.

You are not being accused of anything just yet, Queen Usai said. The thoughts of the other Nocturnals buzzed around them for a flickering moment. *I want to know why both of you chose to work for Aoif Deckler. It is not your actions that matter here. It is your intentions.*

To Joah's left, Damien nodded pointedly at Misla, his warning like a faint breeze. Misla cleared her throat. The Nocturnals around her recoiled from the sound.

I can't speak for my partner here, she said, *but I wanted to talk to the Infected— the bilingual, if you will—to find out what made them leave their homes. I've always been horrified that we behead the Infected when we bring them back. I wanted to change things.*

The truth of her words shivered around the ring. The fire flared. Joah's mind bounced back to their conversation right before they had met the scavengers. He hoped the Nocturnals could access this memory to verify Misla's authenticity. Maybe *she* could escape with Damien, even if they threw Joah back into the twisted prison cells next to Hickory.

And what of you, Joah Cadshaw? Queen Usai asked after a crackling moment of silence. *Why did you become a retriever?*

Joah glanced at Misla, who nodded encouragingly. He swallowed.

Well, my granddad was a retriever. Even as he thought it, he knew this was not enough. He closed his eyes, allowed himself to sink into a cavernous honesty that he had never voiced aloud. *It's easy to believe in a day and night, okay? A darkness and a light. After I was fired—after my wife was killed—they put me in a community position. I had to catch the beasts living among us. It was much harder, because they all wore the same faces. But when you're a retriever, it feels good to pinpoint the monsters so easily. I was saving people from darkness.*

He paused.

I didn't know the Eternal Night could contain so much light. I didn't know you glowed.

The firelight was dropping, but those far-off suns winked above them.

I see, Queen Usai said eventually. *Ignorance, then. Not malevolence. What do you think, Damien?*

Damien twisted in his seat to tilt his head at Joah and Misla.

"Will you save my mom if they tell you?" His voice trembled.

"Of course, kid," Joah said automatically. "Of course we'll save your mom."

Damien turned back to the queen and nodded. Queen Usai made a peculiar twirling motion with her fingers, and a deep buzzing drowned out the sounds of popping fire. It became a roar of sound, like blood was thundering through Joah's ears.

Queen Usai dropped her hands. The roar smothered itself into silence.

Very well. I will tell you. I can see now that you didn't know... couldn't possibly have foreseen. Of course you'd think of us as monsters. But you have to abandon that notion now. You must promise to save your people from the darkness, not behind them, but ahead of them.

Yes, Joah and Misla said together, still holding slippery hands.

Good, Queen Usai said. *Here it is, then, what I have been trying to tell your people for nearly sixty years: there is no fissure ahead of you. The High Road remains unbroken.*

No, Joah said. Warning bells clanged in his memory. He saw Aoif's boxy figure bending over the map, his finger touching that vicious red slash. *General Deckler said the scouts—*

Did you talk to the scouts yourselves? Prince Kal asked. *Did you see the fissure with your own eyes? Or did your people jolt into emergency status at the word of one man?*

Joah flinched, but the Nocturnal queen plunged on before he could answer.

I knew Aoif Deckler sixty years ago, when he was a gangly teenager. I know him better than you do. She paused, her earrings rattling ominously. *I know the man still. So trust me when I tell you: the imposter has been planning this since he helped murder your previous general. He is not leading your community to safety. He is leading you straight into a trap.*

And Joah could sense the queen's genuine terror, and he felt Damien tremble beside him, and Misla's fingernails pierced the back of his hands as the dying fire spit feeble sparks into that everlasting night air, and he knew the Nocturnals were right.

Warn you. Got to, Blair's ghost sang in his head.

General Deckler was sending the Sunsetters to their graves.

Read the next installment of "The Nocturnals"
next month in Metaphorosis.

See Mariah Montoya's "The Nocturnals III"
online at Metaphorosis.
If you liked it, leave a comment. Authors love
that!
Remember to subscribe to our e-mail updates so
you'll know when new stories are posted.

Copyright

Title information

Metaphorosis July 2021

ISSN: 2573-136X (online)
ISBN: 978-1-64076-203-9 (e-book)
ISBN: 978-1-64076-204-6 (paperback)

Copyright

Works of fiction

This book contains works of fiction. Characters, dialogue, places, organizations, incidents, and events portrayed in the works are fictional and are products of the author's imagination or used fictitiously. Any resemblance to actual persons, places, organizations, or events is coincidental.

All rights reserved

Moral rights asserted

Each author whose work is included in this book has asserted their moral rights, including the right to be identified as the author of their respective work(s).

Publisher

Metaphorosis

a magazine of speculative fiction

Metaphorosis Magazine is an imprint of Metaphorosis Publishing
Neskowin, OR, USA

Discounts available

Substantial discounts are available for educational institutions, including writing workshops. Discounts are also available for quantity purchases. For details, contact Metaphorosis at metaphorosis.com/about

Metaphorosis Publishing

Metaphorosis offers beautifully written science fiction and fantasy. Our imprints include:

Metaphorosis Magazine
Plant Based Press
Verdage

You can also find us:
@MetaphorosisMag, @MetaphorosisRev, @Metaphorosis
www.facebook.com/metaphorosis

Help keep Metaphorosis running by supporting us at
Patreon.com/metaphorosis

See more about some of our books on the following pages.

Metaphorosis
a magazine of speculative fiction

Metaphorosis is an online speculative fiction magazine dedicated to quality writing. We publish an original story every week, along with author bios, interviews, and notes on story origins.

We also publish monthly print and e-book issues, as well as yearly Best of and Complete anthologies.

Come and see us online at magazine.Metaphorosis.com

Metaphorosis: Best of 2020

The best science fiction and fantasy stories from *Metaphorosis* magazine's fifth year.

Metaphorosis 2020

All the stories from *Metaphorosis* magazine's fifth year. Fifty-two great SFF stories.

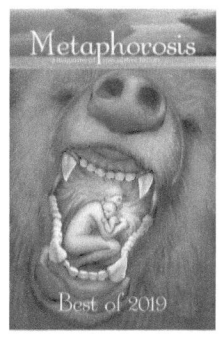

**Metaphorosis:
Best of 2019**

**Metaphorosis
2019**

The best science
fiction and fantasy
stories from
Metaphorosis
magazine's fourth
year.

All the stories
from *Metaphorosis*
magazine's fourth
year. Fifty-two
great SFF stories.

Metaphorosis:
Best of 2018

The best science
fiction and fantasy
stories from
Metaphorosis
magazine's third
year.

Metaphorosis
2018

All the stories
from *Metaphorosis*
magazine's third
year. Fifty-two
great SFF stories.

Metaphorosis:
Best of 2017

The best science
fiction and fantasy
stories from
Metaphorosis
magazine's *second*
year.

Metaphorosis
2017

All the stories
from *Metaphorosis*
magazine's second
year. Fifty-three
great SFF stories.

Metaphorosis: Best of 2016

The best science fiction and fantasy stories from *Metaphorosis* magazine's first year.

Metaphorosis 2016

Almost all the stories from *Metaphorosis* magazine's first year.

Plant Based Press

Vegan-friendly science fiction and fantasy, including an annual anthology of the year's best SFF stories.

Best Vegan SFF of 2020

The best vegan-friendly science fiction and fantasy stories of 2020!

Best Vegan SFF of 2019

The best vegan-friendly science fiction and fantasy stories of 2019!

Best Vegan SFF of 2018

The best vegan-friendly science fiction and fantasy stories of 2018!

Best Vegan SFF of 2017

The best vegan-friendly science fiction and fantasy stories of 2017!

Best Vegan SFF of 2016

The best vegan-friendly science fiction and fantasy stories of 2016!

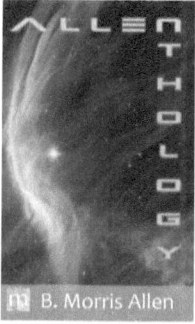

Susurrus

A darkly romantic story of magic, love, and suffering.

Allenthology: Volume I

A quarter century of SFF, including the full contents of the collections *Tocsin, Start with Stones,* and *Metaphorosis.*

Verdage

Science fiction and fantasy books for writers – full of great stories, often with an additional focus on the craft of speculative fiction writing.

Reading 5X5 x2

Duets

How do authors' voices change when they collaborate?

A round-robin of five talented science fiction and fantasy authors collaborating with each other and writing solo.

Including stories by Evan Marcroft, David Gallay, J. Tynan Burke, L'Erin Ogle, and Douglas Anstruther.

Score

an SFF symphony

What if stories were written like music? *Score* is an anthology of varied stories arranged to follow an emotional score from the heights of joy to the depths of despair – but always with a little hope shining through.

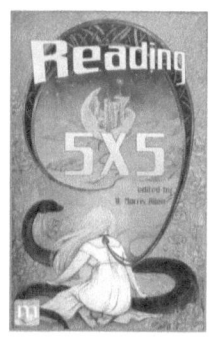 

Reading 5X5

Five stories, five times

Twenty-five SFF authors, five base stories, five versions of each – see how different writers take on the same material.

Reading 5X5

Writers' Edition

Two extra stories, the story seed, and authors' notes on writing. Over 100 pages of additional material specifically aimed at writers.